What a s [barcode: M000190525]

Roxanne decided. How soft and adorable.

Roxanne found her lips puckering of their own accord, and she kissed the baby's downy head. The child stirred, and reluctantly Roxanne put her back into the crib.

But somewhere in her chest she felt her heart constrict, and she wasn't sure why.

Was there some kind of kismet at work at Jake's ranch? Had fate brought her here, to this man and his motherless child, at this particular time and surrounded her with newborn life in order to remind her of something? Something that her old life was missing?

"I get the point," she whispered, "I think I understand...."

Dear Reader,

This June—traditionally the month of brides, weddings and the promise of love everlasting—Silhouette Romance also brings you the possibility of being a star! Check out the details of this special promotion in each of the six happily-ever-afters we have for you.

In *An Officer and a Princess,* Carla Cassidy's suspenseful conclusion to the bestselling series ROYALLY WED: THE STANBURYS, Princess Isabel calls on her former commanding officer to help rescue her missing father. Karen Rose Smith delights us with a struggling mom who refuses to fall for *Her Tycoon Boss* until the dynamic millionaire turns up the heat! In *A Child for Cade* by reader favorite Patricia Thayer, Cade Randall finds that his first love has kept a precious secret from him....

Talented author Alice Sharpe's latest offering, *The Baby Season,* tells of a dedicated career woman tempted by marriage and motherhood with a rugged rancher and his daughter. In *Blind-Date Bride,* the second book of Myrna Mackenzie's charming twin duo, the heroine asks a playboy billionaire to ward off the men sent by her matchmaking brothers. And a single mom decides to tell the man she has always loved that he has a son in Belinda Barnes's heartwarming tale, *The Littlest Wrangler.*

Next month be sure to return for two brand-new series— the exciting DESTINY, TEXAS by Teresa Southwick and the charming THE WEDDING LEGACY by Cara Colter. And don't forget the triumphant conclusion to Patricia Thayer's THE TEXAS BROTHERHOOD, along with three more wonderful stories!

Happy Reading!

Mary-Theresa Hussey

Mary-Theresa Hussey
Senior Editor

Please address questions and book requests to:
Silhouette Reader Service
U.S.: 3010 Walden Ave., P.O. Box 1325, Buffalo, NY 14269
Canadian: P.O. Box 609, Fort Erie, Ont. L2A 5X3

The Baby Season

ALICE SHARPE

Published by Silhouette Books

America's Publisher of Contemporary Romance

This book is dedicated to all the babies in my life: those in
the past, those right now and those to come. I love you all.

A special thanks to Jennifer Jones, Jo Mentzer
and Mary Shumate for sharing their time and expertise.

 SILHOUETTE BOOKS

ISBN 0-373-19525-7

THE BABY SEASON

Copyright © 2001 by Alice Sharpe

Visit Silhouette at www.eHarlequin.com

Printed in U.S.A.

ALICE SHARPE

met her husband-to-be on a cold, foggy beach in Northern California. One year later they were married. Their union has survived the rearing of two children, a handful of earthquakes registering over 6.5, numerous cats and a few special dogs, the latest of which is a yellow Lab named Annie Rose. Alice and her husband now live in a small rural town in Oregon, where she devotes the majority of her time to pursuing her second love, writing.

Alice loves to hear from readers. You can write her at P.O. Box 755, Brownsville, OR 97327. SASE for reply is appreciated.

Chapter One

After three grueling hours, the hike Roxanne Salyer had approached as a means of finding help revealed itself for what it really was: a trek into an inferno.

She should have stayed near her car instead of taking off on foot. Not inside, but near it.

Her car, the victim of the successful attempt to avoid running over a rabbit, was far behind her now, gobbled up by the California desert. Roxanne knew it was up to her to save herself, and if she had to do it wearing half a wilted linen suit and sandals never intended to tackle sand, then so be it.

All in all, not an auspicious beginning to her quest.

A niggling little voice in the back of her head balked at the word *quest* and inserted instead *fool's errand*.

"Oh, give it a rest," she told that voice as she scanned miles and miles of rolling sandy hills and hazy distant mountains. Sporadic poles strung with wire announced the possibility of civilization, but it sure wasn't visible from where she stood. No buildings, no phone booths, no nothing.

Didn't anyone ever drive down this blasted road?

For the first time, fear, and not just annoyance, prickled her overheated skin. People were known to die out in the desert. It happened.

She should have worn less impressive and more durable clothing; she should have carried more water; she should have been prepared.

A big lump suddenly materialized in her throat. She couldn't swallow it—she didn't have enough saliva left. There was nothing to do but continue walking, which she did until her fried brain registered the fact that the road had split in two. One track continued in a more or less straight line, the other curved off to the west, leading to the same mountains, only closer.

Two roads, neither looking well traveled. It was a Robert Frost nightmare.

Her gut said the straight road was the right road but her gut didn't have a great track record. Not today anyway. "West," she muttered, vaguely comforted by the fact that the Pacific Ocean lay in that direction, albeit a hundred miles away.

That's when the strap on her left sandal snapped in two.

She stood for a moment on her right foot, her throat as dry as the sandy earth burning through the thin sole.

Now what?

Jack Wheeler frowned at the sight of the white compact abandoned halfway across his access road. Bumping over small rocks and tumbleweed, he pulled around the car, coming to a stop amidst a billowing cloud of sandy dust. He popped open his door and jumped to the ground, both boots hitting the road at the same time.

As he approached the car, he noticed it sported a Washington State license plate and a sticker on the front bumper advocating the practice of random acts of kindness. He couldn't imagine whom the car belonged to; he wasn't expecting anyone from Washington. He impatiently strode to the driver's door and, using one of his gloves as a makeshift pot holder, tried the handle.

Locked. Leaning down and gazing inside, he spied on the passenger seat an empty bottle of water, a sky-blue woman's jacket, a cell phone and a plastic folder with an unfamiliar logo: a stylized raindrop, inside of which were call letters.

A wave of irritation flashed across the stern contours of his lips. *Oh, brother, not another reporter, radio or otherwise.*

Maybe just a curiosity seeker.

The logo suggested otherwise.

Jack recalled the last big-city reporter who had tried to cozy her way into the tattered remains of his dignity. He'd caught on to her act just in time, but it hadn't saved him from her half-truths.

But that had been right after Nicole left, when the public's curiosity about the whole affair was still white-hot. Besides, this car was parked in a weird spot for a thrill seeker or a writer. It was way too far from the house to see anything, too far from the mountains to provide cover.

Kneeling, he looked under the vehicle and saw a puddle of black fluid and a jagged piece of lava rock, which explained a lot but still left the question: Where was the driver?

He didn't have time for this, he thought with an impatient glance at the pocket watch his father had left him. He was running behind schedule.

It didn't matter. You couldn't leave someone stranded out in the desert. Not even if that someone was a reporter.

On the other hand, he couldn't leave this car partially blocking the road, either. Swearing under his breath, he flattened out on his stomach and dislodged the rock—no easy feat. Then he took a rope from the back of his truck and looped it around first his hitch, then the car fender. Within a few minutes, the automobile sat harmlessly off to the side, tucked up against a sandbank.

Back in the truck, Jack drove north until he hit the fork in the road. It occurred to him that only someone who knew about the studio would stray from the main road, but he stopped anyway and grabbed a pair of small binoculars from the glove compartment.

The desert heat rippled like airborne ocean waves as he scanned the trek leading to the house and found it empty. Next he tried the west road. Was that a figure up ahead? If he or she was from the car, they'd walked almost five miles. Setting aside the binoculars, Jack gunned the engine and swore under his breath.

Another reporter on her way to snoop around the abandoned studio?

Whoever it was would soon regret their decision to invade his privacy.

A few minutes later, he slowed the truck and gaped at the apparition in front of him. Irritation turned to amazement as he took in the figure of a young woman, her expression just as startled as he supposed his was.

She was tall and willowy, with long, dark blond hair caught in a high ponytail, sunglasses perched on a straight nose, wearing what once must have been a silky white blouse and a perfectly cut light blue skirt. Both articles were covered with a film of dust. The sunburn on her throat and arms extended down two shapely pantyhose-free legs. Her right foot was just barely embraced by a delicate white sandal that looked as alien out here on the desert plateau as an ice cream parlor would look in hell, and on her left foot, she wore…a purse.

That demanded a double take and he gave it one. Sure

enough, the woman had stuffed her left foot into a straw shoulder bag. A long strap extended upward, clutched tightly in her left hand. As he stared, she started hobbling toward him, the purse acting as a makeshift shoe.

He jumped out of the truck, a canteen in his hand. As she drew closer, she tried smiling but it apparently hurt because she winced. In that instant, he realized that under the sunburn and the dust she was pretty. Okay, extremely pretty. His defenses immediately went back on to full alert.

"Who *are* you?" he heard himself bark.

This stopped her in her tracks.

He knew he should show compassion—she looked miserable. Even if she was a reporter, she wasn't in the best of straits right now. But what he felt was alarm as he registered how, one by one, his traitorous senses were springing back to life. Even the air had a new sharp smell, and the sun, hitting the back of his neck, felt warmer than it had in two years.

"What are you doing out here?" he grumbled, reminding himself that this woman was definitely *not* his type. He liked small women with fluffy hair. He liked women with more curves, and most importantly, if she was indeed a reporter, he liked women who didn't get their kicks out of snooping into a person's life.

"Didn't you see the No Trespassing signs?" he added.

She gasped, "Is that water?"

He finally got his act together enough to twist off the cap and hand her the canteen, which she immediately upended. He watched her greedily gulping the precious fluid, her throat rippling, water dribbling down her chin, plopping onto her pink bosom and running in tiny rivulets between her breasts, down under the clinging fabric of her shirt.

Jack swallowed hot dry air. "Who are you?" he repeated as she finally lowered the canteen.

"Roxanne Salyer," she said breathlessly. She wiped the

back of her hand across her mouth, smearing the fine coat
of dust into a minor mud slide.

"Is that your car back there?"

She nodded and tried to return the canteen.

"Go ahead and keep it," he told her, handing her the
cap, "but take smaller sips." He studied her for a second,
his gaze eventually drifting down to her unusual footwear.
"Are you hurt?"

Her eyes followed his. She bit her lip and winced again.
All she said was, "My shoe broke."

"Any cramps? Dizziness? Are you nauseous?"

"No, no, honestly, I'm fine. Just really glad to see you."

Her voice was as rich and warm as spiced honey. She
spoke as though greeting a friend after a long absence,
which he supposed wasn't too surprising as she was apparently lost out in the desert and must view him as a savior
of sorts. Ha!

"What are you doing out here?"

"I came to find a woman."

Not so lost after all, and he felt a flush of disappointment
he was hard put to understand. She was looking for a
woman, huh? Two guesses who that might be, and the second one didn't count. Just as he'd thought, she was here
after a story about Nicole. Or—shudder—him! He said, "I
see. Well, my ex-wife is long gone, or don't you do your
own research?"

Roxanne wrinkled her nose which reminded him of his
daughter, Ginny. "She's gone?"

"Yes," he said, leveling her with an icy stare. "Nicole
ran off with the artist I hired to paint her portrait. Last I
heard, they were in France. I have a hard time believing
you find any of this a surprise. What's your game? What
tabloid are you working for? Or is it a radio station? Who
are you?"

She was shaking her head. "I don't work for radio or a tabloid. I work for a television station—"

"You what? Now just a moment. My private life isn't fodder for some sleazy—"

"I work for a network affiliate in Seattle, Washington," she interrupted. "I haven't the slightest idea who you are. I don't know anything about your wife. In other words, we can't possibly be talking about the same woman. Mine is about sixty years old. Her name is Dolly Aames."

The television thing had rattled him. For one awful moment, he had envisioned his sorry life story spread over one of those nighttime exposition shows. Why couldn't Nicole have run off with someone less well-known than Jeremy Titus, heartthrob artist to the stars?

On the offensive again, he barked, "You could have gotten into real trouble wandering around out here."

"I know, I know. Do you have a cell phone I can borrow?"

"Not on me. I saw one in your car."

"It's dead." She looked flustered and edgy as she added, "I used the last of the battery to call my insurance agent. He told me I'm too far away and should call a local towing service. Helpful of him, wasn't it?"

All this was interesting in its own perverse way, but he was running late. Turning on his heel, he said, "Come on, I'll give you a lift to a phone. You can call a tow truck."

"Wait, wait," she said, limping along behind him. "Do you know Dolly Aames?"

"Never heard of her," he said, opening the passenger door. As Roxanne paused beside him, he noticed the scalp exposed by the part in her hair was as sunburned as the rest of her. She was going to be in pain—soon, too. He reached into the glove box and came up with a battered bottle of aspirin. Shaking out a couple, he handed them to her. "Take these now. For your sunburn."

She swallowed the aspirin before climbing past him into the truck. "Shade," she whispered reverently. Hugging the canteen to her chest with one hand and lifting her sunglasses with the other, she glanced down at him. "Heaven," she sighed.

He'd expected blue eyes. What with her fair skin and blond hair, her eyes should have been blue. But Roxanne's eyes were chocolate brown, deep, sensuous, eyes that seemed to absorb the world, eyes that looked kind and full of humor and intelligence. Dangerous eyes.

"Thanks," she said.

He nodded brusquely as he slammed her door. Pulling his hat off his head and putting it back on again, he walked around to his own door, his stride purposeful as he attempted to stuff this woman's abrupt appearance in his life into a tiny cupboard under his mental stairs.

Trouble was, it was already pretty crowded in there....

It wasn't until the truck was headed in the opposite direction that Roxanne began to relax. Well, that wasn't totally true, she realized. It was a little impossible to relax with the surly stranger sitting beside her taunting every square inch of her parched flesh.

At first, standing in the road, aware that a vehicle was approaching in a cloud of dust, she'd felt tremendous relief. She was to escape an ignominious demise after all. Hallelujah!

But the tall man who jumped out of the truck had startled her with his intensity, with the way his blazing blue gaze had raked her from head to toe, with the twist of his lips as he studied her face and the timbre of his voice as he barked questions. It wasn't until she registered the canteen in his hand that she was able to mutter anything.

Glancing over at his profile now, she wondered if she dared impose on him further for lip balm, and decided on a long drink of water instead. The sight of him concentrating on the empty road ahead did nothing to soothe her—quite the contrary. Her heart felt like it was beating double time.

"I don't know your name," she said.

He flicked her a short glance. "Jack Wheeler." What he saw apparently didn't please him because he looked away at once, his brow set in a frown.

It was obvious the handsome stranger didn't much care for rescuing damsels in distress. Well, she didn't much like being said damsel.

Jack looked as though he was about a decade older than her, in his mid- to late thirties. His skin was tanned a warm brown color. No wedding ring, no tan line where one had ever been. His short brown hair was sun-bleached and nearly hidden under a worn Stetson. A battered tan work shirt and equally disreputable blue jeans with leather gloves stuffed in a hip pocket completed his ensemble. His facial features were strong, though perhaps this was just an impression helped along by what appeared to be his habitual expression of weary tolerance.

Judging from his worn clothes and the coils of barbed wire she'd glimpsed in the back of the truck, she decided he was a rancher, perhaps with local connections in politics. No itinerant cowboy would be so worried that a newspaper or tabloid had come a-callin'.... Besides, he'd mentioned commissioning an artist to paint his wife's portrait.

The desert was probably littered with men like him, she thought. Disillusioned men who had somehow lost what they once had.

Like a wife.

Maybe the missus got tired of living out in the middle of nowhere, even if it was with Jack Wheeler who looked more than capable of providing enough nighttime stimuli to keep the old hearth fires burning.

Her heart fluttered a little with the thought of this man starting fires only he could extinguish. All that energy, all that power, all that size—the thought of him leaning in close to her, of running those brown fingers along her face, down her spine—it sent chills racing across her overheated skin.

It was kind of impossible not to compare this hunk of he-man flesh with the refined presence of her former boyfriend, Kevin, a news anchor at the station where they both worked. Four days earlier, he'd dumped her, flashing all twenty-eight perfectly capped teeth as he smiled like a used car salesman and spat out the hated words, "Face it, Roxanne. You're just like your mother."

Good riddance, she'd said, but his words had stung.

She put aside thoughts of Kevin and moved along to the next puzzle: a pink box tied with a pink ribbon sitting on the bench seat between them. Utterly feminine, the box implied a new love interest, which made Roxanne so curious it was all she could do to mind her own business.

Business reminded her why she was there. "I'm looking for Dolly Aames," she declared once again.

"So you said."

"Last anyone heard from her, she lived out here—"

"Listen," he said, cutting her short, "this is the desert. A really remote part of the desert."

"Not that remote, not by car. Not even half an hour from town if you stay in your car—"

"If your friend lived out here and let connections back home drop," he said, interrupting her with another flick of his blue eyes, "then I'd be the last person in the world to blow her cover. I've never heard of her. Honest."

"But you wouldn't tell me even if you had?"

"No."

"Then how do I know you're not lying now?"

He shrugged. "I guess you don't."

About then, they hit the fork in the road. He turned in the direction Roxanne had decided against.

"Where was I headed?" she asked.

"You don't know?"

She gestured at her foot, slipping the purse off as she did so. How embarrassing to have a man like this come across her with her foot stuffed in a purse! Digging in her skirt pockets, she extracted the car keys, wallet and micro tape recorder she'd deposited there when her shoe broke. At the sight of the tape recorder, Jack grimaced.

"What's that for?" he demanded.

She held up the little contraption. "This?"

"Yeah. Who do you plan to record?"

"Dolly Aames, of course," she said, throwing her belongings back in the now-tattered bag where they belonged.

"You should never have turned off the main highway," he said, his voice as dry as the landscape. "This is all private property out here. It belongs to the High W Ranch. It's well marked."

"I didn't see any signs," she told him truthfully, but she suspected that even if she had, she would have taken a chance.

He grunted.

Roxanne indulged in more canteen water. Would a little tin sign nailed to a fence have dissuaded her from turning off the main road and trying to fulfill her grandmother's fondest wish? Not likely!

"The signs are there," he said firmly.

"But I didn't see them. How can this be a ranch? I don't see a single cow. Even if there are cows, what do they eat?"

"I'm still having trouble imagining someone dressed as inappropriately as you are striking out on her own," he said, obviously not interested in discussing what the cows ate. "You should have carried water and stayed near your car. At the very least, you could have used your jacket to shade your head. If you were going to walk, then why not head back out to the highway? If I hadn't come along..."

His voice trailed off. Even though she had thought the very same things, his observations made her bristle. "I'm sorry if I just flunked your version of Desert Survival 101. I'm new at this. I knew the highway was a long way back. The mountains looked closer. Besides, *that* was the direction I needed to go."

Digging in her pocket, she extracted a yellowed envelope. "Dolly Aames," she said evenly, "sent this letter to my grandmother almost forty years ago. See, the postmark on the envelope says Tangent, January, 1964."

He stopped the truck in the middle of the empty road, then turned to her. Face on, within the tight confines of the truck cab, his presence was overwhelming and she gulped.

"Let me get this straight. You're trying to track down a woman no one has heard from in forty years? What are you, a private eye? A bounty hunter?"

"I told you, I work for a television affiliate in Seattle. I produce midday news programming."

"Produce? I would have thought you'd be in front of the camera."

"The real power is behind the camera."

"Power, huh? You're one of those."

"No, I'm not one of those. I just enjoy putting things together. Besides, I hate makeup, and have more bad hair days than good ones. Now, about Dolly Aames..."

His gaze traveled up to her hair and back again. She could only guess its current condition, but as he didn't sputter a rebuttal, she imagined the worst. "Is this woman an escaped criminal or a notorious husband killer?" he asked.

"Of course not."

"Then why did you come all the way from Seattle to find her? Is she a relative?"

"No. She's an old friend of my grandmother's."

"So you traveled almost two thousand miles just to look up an old friend of the family? Why did your grandmother wait so many years to look for her?"

"It's complicated," Roxanne said, hedging. She didn't want to go into the details of her grandmother's illness just to satisfy this guy's curiosity. Besides, she could barely stand to think about Grandma Nell's symptoms and what they might portend. She added, "Grandma wants to reunite a singing group they both belonged to a long time ago."

"And how about you? What do you want?"

She stared at him, unblinking, then muttered, "I want to help my grandmother."

"Hmm—" Shaking his head he added, "Has it occurred to either one of you that this Dolly either moved away or died?"

"Of course. But you have to start somewhere."

He shook his head. "Well, I think that's pretty incredible. And very naive."

Opening the envelope, she took out a small, faded photograph of a young woman standing next to a fence. Each rustic post was topped with the bleached skull of a longhorn, making it a rather grisly, if unique, setting. She shoved it under his nose.

He took it reluctantly.

"I stayed in Tangent last night and asked around town— not that it did me much good because most everything was already closed when I got there. Anyway, no one knew Dolly Aames, but the guy at the motel said this photo was taken at the juncture of this road and the highway. He told me how to get out here."

"Was that Pete at the Cactus Gulch or Alan over at the Midtown?"

"I guess it was Pete. I just stayed there one night and

checked out this morning. I can't believe you know his name.''

''It's a very small town,'' Jack said, handing the photo back. ''Okay, I'll grant you that this photo was taken here, more or less. Those skulls were something of a landmark for a long time until I got rid of them. Still, people came from miles around to pose with the damn things, so I don't see that the photo means anything. I don't know who Dolly Aames is.''

''Hmm—''

''Maybe Sal will,'' he said slowly, as though hesitant to admit he might have a way of helping.

''Really? Who's Sal?''

''Sally Collins, but you're a braver soul than I if you call her Sally instead of Sal. I have to warn you though, she's not quite as forthcoming about these things as I am.''

''You're forthcoming? You've got to be kidding.''

He cast her a serious look. ''Roxanne, has it ever occurred to you that Dolly Aames may not want to be found?''

No, as a matter of fact it hadn't.

Chapter Two

The house within the rolling hills turned out to be a sprawling white stucco structure with a red tile roof. Desert plants brought to life by vivid spills of flowers enhanced the aura of an oasis. Only a huge helium-filled bouquet of pink and white balloons tied to an old-fashioned pump provided a jarring note.

"Is this your place? It's gorgeous."

He cast her a speculative look as he circled the house and parked in front of a small barn. Next to it was another wooden building, this one long and low with a split-rail corral attached to one side. Within the corral were two horses who ambled over to the fence to stare at the truck and its passengers.

"Aren't they cute?" she said. "What are their names?"

"The pregnant white mare is called Sprite and the bay gelding is Milo," he said with a sidelong glance at her.

When Jack got out of the truck, the brown horse whinnied and the white horse tossed her head and snorted. After running a hand along their sleek necks, Jack reached back into the truck and snagged the pink box, keeping a firm grip on it in his large hand. His gaze met Roxanne's, and he produced a shy grin.

It looked good on him, she decided. He really should try doing it more often.

This thought was cut short when a side door on the barn opened and out walked a large man with rounded shoulders. He wore a hat much like Jack's though his was black and crisp instead of crumpled and dusty.

The newcomer slapped his leg and a shaggy black-and-white dog appeared.

Jack slammed his door. "Carl, this is Roxanne. How's the new filly?"

Carl nodded his greeting, his gaze lingering on Roxanne's face a moment longer than was necessary. Roxanne touched her cheek. Her fingers came away gritty.

"She's doing great," Carl said. "What about the south fence?"

"Fixed for now, but Monday morning you'll have to get the boys to make it more permanent."

Jack looked toward the house, then back at Roxanne, as though trying to decide something. Finally he said, "I'd like to check on the new filly. Do you want to see her?"

What Roxanne wanted was a phone, more water and a clue to Dolly Aames's location. But Jack was watching her with a question in his eyes and it was impossible not to respond. "Sure," she said.

He opened the barn door and entered, followed by Carl. Roxanne limped past him, watching the ground for rocks that might gouge her bare foot.

The barn was cool, narrow and deeply shadowed, smelling pleasantly of hay and horses. There were four stalls, a stack of bales at the far end and a smattering of equine paraphernalia hanging from walls and dividers. Only one stall was occupied. A palomino mare and her foal glanced at the humans with obvious curiosity.

"Ah, now, isn't she sweet?" Jack said softly, draping himself over the gate and petting the mare's velvet muzzle, his eyes on the baby. "There you go, Goldy. You got yourself a real beauty this time."

The mare snorted and sniffed and managed to look proud of her offspring. The youngster stayed back by her mother's flank, as though bashful.

Roxanne's impatience with this diversion dissipated as her television producer instincts kicked in—babies of any kind sold a story.

The image of this little filly, for instance, and the strong, good-looking guy hanging on the fence admiring her, was great. Even the shadowed stall and the glint of sunlight from the open door spilling across the hay-scattered floor would come alive on the screen.

As for Jack? Well, besides an interesting face and eyes to die for, he had broad shoulders tapering down to a trim waist, and an absolutely top-rate denim-clad rear end. Add the way he moved, kind of long legged, and the way he spoke, kind of warm but with an edge, and you had a man captivating enough to interest any female with a pulse.

Even the hat was perfect. Crushed, dusty, sexy as all get out, especially when Jack peered from under the brim with those laser-blue eyes.

She wondered if her boss would be interested in a story about modern cowboys. Maybe they could dig up a few cows to lend credibility...

The mare nosed Roxanne's arm, making her jump about six inches in the air and cutting short her reverie. She must have made a startled sound, because she heard one. The two men stared at her with raised eyebrows and twitching lips.

"This is the closest I've ever been to a horse," she mumbled.

"Really?" Jack said. The filly moved toward his outstretched hand, and he ran his fingers through the tufts of her sprouting mane.

"How old is the baby horse?"

Jack and Carl exchanged quick glances. Finally Jack said, "About twelve hours. Goldy always births in the wee hours of the morning."

The baby was the same color as the straw, lighter than her mother. She had a white blaze running down her face and one white sock on her front left leg. Roxanne said, "She's just the most darling thing I've ever seen."

"The second most darling," Jack said, and glancing up at him, she found him looking at her. Wait a second now... Was he saying that *she* was more darling than this horse? Was that a compliment?

For a second, she lost herself in the pure blue of his eyes, amazed he would express such a tender sentiment—assuming that comparing a woman to a horse was indeed tender—after knowing her such a short time. No, amazed wasn't the right word. Dazzled, perhaps. Intrigued. Breathless.

Stunned.

He was the most impressive guy she'd ever met, hands down, flat-out mesmerizing.

What about Kevin?

Kevin who?

But the moment passed and it dawned on her that his gaze was really fixed on the open door. She turned to see what he found so fascinating, and discovered he hadn't been talking about her at all. A very small girl stood just inside the barn. She was wearing denim overalls, a pink shirt and matching pink shoes. Her yellow hair was wound up into two blond pigtails that glowed with the sunlight behind her. And she was undoubtedly adorable.

"Daddy!" she screeched, running at Jack with open arms.

The commotion unsettled the jittery new mother horse, who snorted, stamped a foot and turned in her stall. The baby whinnied and turned, too.

Jack caught the child and swung her up on his hip. "Shh," he said. "You're frightening Goldy."

"And the baby," the child said with a lisp.

"Yes, and the baby."

"Is that mine?" she asked, pointing at the pink box in Jack's hand.

"Yes, but not until your party."

The little girl finally noticed Roxanne. She buried her head against her father's shoulder, revealing just one blue eye, which she fixed on Roxanne's face.

Roxanne smiled and the child completely buried her head. Roxanne wasn't surprised. This was not only her first experience with a small horse, but also with a small human. She'd probably frightened the poor little thing.

"This is my daughter, Ginny," Jack said, looking from Roxanne to his child. "Ginny, this lady's name is Roxanne."

"Hello, Ginny," Roxanne said in her best put-a-child-at-ease voice. "Is it your birthday?"

Ginny pushed her head away from her father's chest and produced a grin that looked just like her father's. "Yes," she said holding up three pudgy fingers.

Jack said, "Hey, pumpkin, how are Aggie's puppies doing?"

"Good."

He tickled her and she wiggled to the ground. With another shy glance up at Roxanne, the child said, "Wanna see?"

"The puppies?" Roxanne said.

"No." Pressing one small finger against her lips and whispering, she added, "It's a secret."

Roxanne felt like scratching her head. The puppies were a secret? From whom?

"I think I know what she means," Jack said as they both watched the little girl make her way across the barn to an empty stall, glancing back over her shoulder at them periodically. "Follow me," he added.

Jack walked into an empty stall, Roxanne right behind him, watching her step. The straw might look innocent, but she'd found it poked at her tender city toes if she stepped on it wrong. Ginny was halfway up a stack of bales, scrambling at such a pace it was obvious she was experienced at this kind of thing. Jack climbed a couple, and reaching down, took Roxanne's hand and pulled her up beside him. She teetered a second, and his grip tightened. A totally unexpected shiver ran up her arm.

"You okay?"

"Just not used to climbing around in the hay."

"Shall I keep hold of your hand or are you steady now?"

"Oh, I'm steady," she said as he dropped her hand. The truth was that she was anything but. His touch had spurted up her arm like a fizzing fuse. She was loathe to have him take his hand away, but even more concerned that he should sense this.

What was going on? She felt kind of dizzy. Perhaps it was the effects of dehydration.

They climbed up beside Ginny who motioned for Roxanne and her dad to take a look. Roxanne peered over Ginny's bent head into a crevice formed between the bales, and found six faces staring back.

Kittens.

One orange, two black, a gray-and-white, a pure white and a tabby. Little meows. Tiny little pink tongues and blurry bluish eyes.

"Go ahead, touch one," Jack said as he gently stroked a tiny white-and-pink ear.

"Oh, I couldn't," Roxanne said. They looked far too fragile to touch. Jack seemed to know what he was doing, but his finger looked huge next to the kitten's head.

Pointing at each kitten in turn, Ginny said, "Blinky and Fuzzy and Foggy and Casper and Blackie and George."

Just then, the mother cat appeared at Ginny's elbow and jumped down into the crevice. As she flopped onto her side, the kittens, meowing in earnest now, jockeyed for position until everyone was lined up with their own nipple and settled in for lunch.

The cat, purring, began bathing her offspring.

"Isn't motherhood something?" Jack said.

"I wouldn't know," Roxanne mumbled. Motherhood wasn't something she spent a lot of time thinking about. Out of nowhere, she heard Kevin's voice again, telling her this very thing just four days earlier.

Jack turned his attention to his daughter. "Okay, sweetpea, time to leave Flossy and her babies alone. And remember, don't tell Aggie."

"'Cause it's a secret."

"That's right."

As Ginny scrambled down the stack, Roxanne said, "The kittens are a secret from the dog?"

He shrugged. "Not really, but little kids love secrets."

Ginny was back on the floor within seconds, Jack right after her, Roxanne slowly following. Jack took her hand again and steadied her last few steps to the ground.

By now, Ginny was running out the door. Jack released Roxanne's hand. She gestured for him to go after his daughter, happy to have a moment to collect what was left of her wits.

"That Ginny is one sweet little kid, isn't she?" Carl said, emerging from a stall with a bucket of grain.

Roxanne jumped at the sound of his voice—she hadn't realized he was still in the barn. "What? Oh, yes. Adorable." For a second, she thought of the little pink-and-blond child and actually felt a smile tug at her lips. She'd had no idea little girls were so...well, cute.

Vaguely uncomfortable with her gut reaction to Carl's remark, she added, "Carl, have you lived out here long?"

"All my life."

"Ever hear of a woman called Dolly Aames? She'd be about sixty now. I know she lived in this area forty or so years ago. Maybe right here in this very house."

He straightened up and scratched his fleshy chin. "The Wheeler family has been here longer than that," he said. "Jack's grandfather built the house. Sorry, but I don't remember anyone by that name ever living here."

It was getting to be a familiar refrain. "Thanks, anyway. Jack said I could use the phone."

"Sure thing. Come on into the house," Carl said.

As she hobbled across the yard beside Carl, she said, "This place is really beautiful."

"It *is* nice," he said with a fond smile. "'Course, what with Doc's schedule, all the heavy work falls to me and the other hands, but that's the way I like it. Been here long enough now that the place feels like home. Know what I mean?"

She decided to ignore his question about home—it made her feel funny inside, the way he phrased it. Home? Home was where you slept, where you paid rent, where you got dressed in the morning to go to work. She said, "Doc?"

"The guy you rode in with."

"Jack Wheeler?"

"Sure. Only almost everyone calls him Doc Wheeler, just like his dad before him."

Roxanne glanced ahead to find Jack standing on a rock porch. He seemed to be studying her as she hobbled along, his expression hovering somewhere between anxious and…unreadable. She didn't know why she made him look like that. His daughter didn't. His horses didn't. Not even Carl did.

She suddenly found herself wanting to make him relax and maybe even grin, and she racked her brain for something funny to say.

Nothing came to her.

She tried a smile.

He nodded politely while holding out a cordless phone, then he spoke to Carl. "People are going to start arriving soon. Maybe we'd better convince Aggie that she and her pups would be happier out in the barn. It's about time for them to move anyway."

Carl nodded and disappeared into the house.

Roxanne took the phone. She was about to ask for a phone book when Jack met her gaze and rattled off a number. She punched it in, got an answering machine saying that Oz, of Oz Repair and Towing, was out on a job, leave a name and number, he'd get back to you. She found a number on the phone and left it on Oz's answering machine along with her name and on second thought, Jack Wheeler's name.

"Looks as though you're stuck with me for a while," she told Jack.

He grunted. "Oz can be a little…unpredictable. He's got things going on at home, too. He'll get back to you, all right, only on his own time schedule." He stared at her for an eternity and added, "We're having a party for Ginny. I need to shower and change clothes before the guests arrive."

"She's very charming," Roxanne said.

Now his face softened again. The man was obviously a sucker for his kid. Roxanne found that rather intriguing. She couldn't imagine either of her parents going out of their way to host a birthday party for her at such a tender age...okay, at any age.

"I can't believe she's already three years old," Jack said.

It suddenly occurred to Roxanne that Jack's wife hadn't only abandoned him but their child. How incredible! Having made the decision to have a baby, how could the woman then abandon her?

On the other hand, how could she abandon Jack Wheeler?

She said, "Carl said you're a doctor. What kind?"

"General practitioner. I have a little office in Tangent. I'm one of a dying breed of small-town doctors. I do everything from tending to the dying to delivering babies."

"Delivering babies," she mumbled. "Why am I not surprised?"

"Listen," he said, obviously trying to figure out what to do with Roxanne. "A kid's party is going to be boring as hell for you."

"I don't mind."

"It's a big house. There are plenty of places to relax until Oz calls back."

"Will there be any adults at the party?"

"Yes—"

"From around here?"

"Of course."

"Maybe one of them will know something about Dolly Aames," Roxanne said. "Would you mind if I invite myself to your party?"

He looked her up and down. Until that moment, she wasn't even aware she knew how to blush, but under his scrutiny, imagining what a mess she was, she felt her cheeks grow warm. Maybe it was just the blasted sunburn catching up with her.

"I could wash first," she said. "And maybe borrow a shoe."

He looked unconvinced that washing or shoes would help her appearance. How he managed to suffuse this skeptical expression with enough sexual energy to rival a nuclear power plant was fascinating and would require further contemplation on Roxanne's part.

But not now.

Now she was too busy inviting herself to a child's party....

"You're welcome to come," he said.

"And what about Sal? Will she be there?"

"Yes. Sal will be there and you can ask her about Dolly Aames. You're persistent, aren't you?"

"I am indeed," Roxanne said.

Carl reappeared just then, loaded down with a box. A glance inside showed four black-and-white puppies. The mom was the shaggy black-and-white dog who was now hanging around down by Carl's knees, casting him worried looks. "I'll settle them in the barn and then I'll see to the barbecue and the ice."

"Thanks, Carl," Jack said. Holding the door for Roxanne, he added, "This way."

The door opened into a large, square kitchen with rough ceiling beams. Long windows faced away from the sun and the room was cool even though Roxanne detected no air-conditioning. There were reddish tiles on the floors, the drain boards were made of thick wooden planks and were covered with several bowls of salad, platters of meat, cheese and vegetables, stacks of sandwiches and a pink birthday cake.

It was a gorgeous room filled with delectable smells that reminded Roxanne she was hungry. Starving. She wondered if she could sneak a cucumber wedge. Or a sandwich. She politely kept her hands to herself as she met the gaze of an attractive woman of about thirty wearing blue jeans and a baggy fringed cowboy shirt. Jack's girlfriend? The woman smiled at Roxanne.

"Roxanne, meet Grace, our housekeeper slash cook," Jack said. "Grace, this is Roxanne."

Grace, who was at the huge stove, was busily stirring a pot of something that smelled good enough to...well, eat...said, "Hi."

"If you have time, could you show Roxanne where to clean up, and maybe loan her something to wear to Ginny's party?"

"Oh, I couldn't impose like that—" Roxanne said, but Grace laughed.

"Trust me, this is one time when you want to impose," she said, her gaze assessing Roxanne. "Besides, it's no bother. This stuff should simmer for a while anyway." With that, she turned down the gas flame under the pot of what smelled like barbecue sauce.

"I'll leave you in capable hands," Jack said with a lingering look that was hard to read. He took off his hat and ran a tanned hand through his short hair, his gaze still fastened on Roxanne, and she had to remind herself to breathe and blink and not gape.

There was something about this man that had her catching her breath like no other man ever had. It wasn't just his startling good looks—she regularly spent her days around men the camera loved, Kevin among them. It was something else, something elusive, something that seemed to charge the air between them that had Roxanne's fertile imagination conjuring up some mighty interesting scenarios. She could almost feel those hands of his running through *her* hair, could almost see his eyes close with passion as his lips touched hers...

He finally shifted his gaze to Grace. "Where did Ginny disappear to?"

"Sal is helping her get ready for her party."

With a last look at Roxanne, Jack left the kitchen, and she watched his retreat with a combination of fascination and lust. Damn, the man looked as good leaving a room as he did entering it!

Grace touched her arm. A glance down at Grace's hand revealed a wedding band, which made Roxanne foolishly happy.

"We have a couple of rooms of our own behind the kitchen," Grace said. "You need a shower and some lotion for that sunburn. Come with me."

"But Sal might know of a woman I'm here to find. Her name is Dolly Aames. Do *you* know anything about her?"

"Nope," Grace said. "I've never heard that name before. I hate to be rude, but now is when I can take a few minutes to get you settled. Later I have to get the chicken ready for the grill and—"

"I'm the one who's rude," Roxanne said. "Of course, I'll talk to Sal later."

Within moments, Grace had shown Roxanne the bathroom, secured a clean towel and washcloth, even produced a toothbrush still wrapped in cellophane. "Help yourself to whatever else you need," she told Roxanne. "Here's lotion with aloe for after your shower. I'll put clothes out on the bed. We're about the same size, more or less. You're in luck—I bought underwear a while ago that I haven't had the occasion to wear. Not likely to any time soon. Holler if you need anything."

As Grace closed the bedroom door behind her, Roxanne came face-to-face with her reflection in the long mirror that backed the door.

"Oh, my," she said.

Her clothes were a wreck, streaked with dirt, splotched with something greasy, covered with tiny pieces of straw. The dry cleaner back home wasn't going to be amused. Her fancy shoe—the one she hadn't broken—was history. And her straw purse looked like something she should donate to the cats in the barn.

Bad as all that was, it couldn't touch what she looked like above the neck. Straw-encrusted hair struggling to escape the ponytail, face sunburned and dirty, crimson and white and brown.

She turned away from the mirror. A cool shower would help. A shower had to help....

She emerged sometime later with tingling pink skin and a mop of wet hair. A glance in the bathroom mirror revealed a face still colorful, but clean. A blow-dryer took care of the hair as long as she was careful to keep it away from her skin. Lotion helped with the burn. She didn't want to use Grace's cosmetics, and her own were still locked in the trunk of her car, so she'd have to go without mascara, her one concession to beauty. She didn't *need* blush she thought with a smile, but when she found a tube of Vaseline, she smeared a little on her finger and gently applied it to her lips, sighing with relief. Heaven!

Wrapped in a towel, she let herself back into Grace's bedroom and found a black dress laid out on the red-and-yellow quilt. Next to it were two pieces of lacy black underwear, the tags still attached.

Roxanne put on the black strapless bra and panties that fit like a second skin. She didn't own any lingerie as beautiful or luxurious—it always seemed silly to spend money on something no one else ever saw.

Not even Kevin, thank the Lord. The swine.

The black rayon dress had an elastic waist and neckline and a full skirt that draped softly to below Roxanne's knees. She cinched it at the waist with an incredible silver-and-turquoise concho belt she found lying beside the dress. She pulled the neckline down off her shoulders and looked in the mirror. Not too bad. Considering everything.

She left her hair loose on her shoulders, slipped her feet

into a pair of Grace's black sandals that were only a little snug and piled her own belongings into a pitiful heap on a chair.

She was ready to look for Sal.

Grace handed Roxanne a glass of iced tea the minute she entered the kitchen. "I knew that dress would look great on you," she said.

"Thanks. I really appreciate the loan. It smells heavenly in here."

"Doc said to remind you to keep drinking fluids and to take a couple more buffered aspirin. I put them out on the counter for you."

As Roxanne swallowed the pills and hoped they would somehow magically make her skin feel less prickly, she said, "I don't suppose Oz called?"

"Nope."

"You waitin' for Oz, you'll be here a while," Carl said as he pushed a wheelbarrow full of blue sacks of crushed ice into the kitchen. He started emptying them one by one into the large bowls that cradled the smaller bowls of perishable food. Looking at Grace, he abandoned his ice and went to stand beside her. "How you feeling, honey?"

"I'm fine," she said.

"You look tired. Maybe Doc should—"

"No, Carl. Now, stop, honey. I'm fine."

They exchanged a lingering look. Roxanne finally noticed that Carl wore a wedding ring identical in design to the one Grace wore.

"I just don't want you overdoing it," he said. "Doc said you have to take it easy this time."

Grace patted his cheek tenderly, lifting a spoon from the pot of bubbling sauce to his lips. "Tell me what it needs."

He tasted. "Salt."

As Grace added a pinch of salt, she glanced at Roxanne

and explained, "I'm pregnant," she said. "I had a miscarriage last year, so we're being extra careful this time."

"Of course. Uh—congratulations."

Beaming, Carl and Grace said, "Thanks," in unison.

As they worked side by side, Roxanne thought to herself that Jack Wheeler's house had a very nice feel to it. How wonderful it must be to grow up with kind people like these, in a house this warm and welcoming, with a father whose eyes flooded with joy when he caught sight of you.

Lucky little Ginny.

Even without a mother?

Well, as Roxanne knew, there was more than one way for a mother to absent herself. Her own upbringing had been adequate but formal. Her mother was fond of saying she just wasn't demonstrative, as though being aloof was a commendable character trait. Roxanne had known she was an "accident" before she had the slightest idea what that meant.

If she ever got married and decided on having children, what kind of mother would she make? Would she be like her own mother or might she be more like her grandmother? The two of them represented opposite ends of the parenting spectrum. One was perpetually annoyed at any inconvenience, one was full of serendipity. One threw money at any problem, the other gave love. How could Roxanne tell what she would be like?

After downing the tea, she rinsed out the glass in the copper sink. "Is there anything I can do to help?"

Carl shook his head as he moved his operation to a large metal kettle filled with cans of soft drinks. Grace said, "No, really, everything is under control. Why don't you go on out? People are beginning to arrive."

Roxanne turned in the direction Grace gestured and saw double French doors. Peering through the glass, she saw a large, enclosed courtyard paved with brick in a herringbone pattern, boasting a bubbling fountain and haphazard pots of flowers. Chairs were clustered around tables heaped with nonperishable food and piles of presents. Two huge creamy umbrellas created shade over half the area. The perimeter was dotted with more doors leading into other rooms and an arch open to the outside. A few people had arrived, and Roxanne searched for a sign of Jack.

Face it, she thought in a moment of truth, she'd been straining for a sight of him or the sound of his voice ever since entering the kitchen. She'd been pleased he'd thought about her sunburn, though she supposed that kind of concern went with being a doctor. Now she scanned the few assembled people. Jack wasn't among them and she fought to hide her disappointment, even from herself.

Was she anxious to show him what lay beneath all the dirt and grime? Did she want to surprise him, intrigue him, the way he'd been surprising and intriguing her from the first moment he rumbled into her life?

"Now, who are you?"

Roxanne turned to find a small woman peering at her. She wore her silver hair cut short around a heavily lined face to which the sun and passing years hadn't been kind.

"I thought I knew all of Jack's friends, but you're a stranger," the woman added.

Roxanne introduced herself.

"I'm Sal. Glad to meet you, Roxy."

Roxanne shook hands as she smiled at the friendly, wrinkled face of the woman staring back at her. All she could think was that this woman had to be close in age to the missing Dolly Aames. If she'd lived here long enough, they would have been peers, maybe even friends. Her mission, which had begun to seem daunting, suddenly came into focus. In a few minutes, she'd hopefully know more about Dolly.

Roxanne explained about her car. "I'm waiting for Oz to call," she added.

"He won't call this afternoon," Sal said, shaking her head. "Lisa is in a state. The twins have colds."

"Oh, I'm sorry to hear that."

"Jack will have to go see them tomorrow."

"You call him Jack? Everyone else seems to call him Doc."

"I helped raise him," she said proudly. "Once you wipe a kid's nose, it's hard to start thinking of him as a grown man."

Roxanne smiled at the image that suddenly sprung before her eyes, of Jack as a child, with a runny nose. Had he looked like his daughter or did his daughter look like his wife? Why did she care? Anxious to get the conversation—and herself—back on track, Roxanne added, "Jack said you might be able to help me. I'm looking for someone."

"Glad to help. I know most everyone in these parts. Bound to after all these years."

"Great. The woman I'm looking for moved to California almost forty years ago. I think she ended up right here or very close by. Of course, she might have married and taken a new last name or moved away entirely. Anyway, I'm trying to find her. Her name is Dolly Aames."

There was a heartbeat when the scant ten inches between the two women suddenly seemed to close to millimeters, then just as abruptly crack open like the Grand Canyon.

Sal blinked rapidly and said, "I've never heard that name. I can't help you." With a decisive nod, she let herself out into the courtyard.

Roxanne narrowed her eyes.

That hesitation had spoken as loud and clear as the sudden blanching of Sal's face.

Sal knew something about Dolly Aames.

Chapter Three

"Duck," Jack said as he entered the courtyard through his bedroom door, Ginny on his shoulders. Ginny giggled as she lowered her head, and once outside, Jack paused for a moment to scan the few faces that had already gathered. No Roxanne.

Good. He wished she had quietly accepted his offer of an out-of-the-way room until Oz got back to her. He toyed around with the idea of having Carl drive her into town, to the motel, where she would be out of sight, out of reach, but he needed Carl here. It's just that he didn't want to see Roxanne Salyer again.

That was the biggest lie he'd told himself in months, and he knew it. The truth of the matter was that he was aching to see her. He could tell himself it was to check on her sunburn, but again, that was a lie. He just wanted to see her, that was all. Cleaned up, he wondered if she'd look all professional like a big-city television producer. Maybe she'd lose that waiflike appearance the desert had forced on her. Maybe she'd be so different that he could find a way to forget he'd ever met her.

After all, she wasn't his type.

Only, what type was she? Sure, her looks were different than the kind of woman who usually got under his skin. But what did looks have to do with anything?

The purely male part of him knew looks had a lot to do with everything. Not just height and weight and coloring, but that inner something that glowed in some women, that seeped through their every little pore and made them iridescent.

Even if their pores were clogged with desert sand?

Even then. Some women had it. Roxanne had it.

Jack mentally slapped himself upside the head. He was thinking like a fool. Still, he couldn't imagine his ex-wife, Nicole, taking the time or trouble to track down a family friend unless there was something in it for her.

Family meant everything to him. Perhaps it came from being an only child, raised out on a ranch, away from town, with parents who doted not only on him but on each other. Some of Jack's first memories were of being about Ginny's age, sitting in the saddle in front of his dad, his mother on her own horse. They'd head up to the mountains where there were a zillion places to picnic with a view as big as the world. Or so it seemed to him.

This memory always flooded him with emotion as it was on this very ride, years later, that his mother's horse had bolted, then stumbled, throwing her to the rocky ground. She'd died within hours. Jack was eight years old at the time, but he could still remember the numbing grief.

Eventually, however, life on the ranch had resumed its contented pace mainly because of Sal. She'd started working at the Wheeler place as a housekeeper. After his mother died, she'd become more important.

After losing his wife, Jack's father had rededicated himself to his role as town doctor. Jack had decided early on to follow in his father's footsteps. He'd envisioned the two of them practicing side by side, and they had for a few years until a stroke claimed his dad. Still, smack in the middle of his career, Jack felt with all his heart that he was doing what he was meant to do.

That and being a good father. Being a father counted—he would always be important to Ginny, she would always be important to him. Man/woman relations, marriage—now that was a different matter. Relationships changed. Nicole had changed.

The marriage should have worked; that's what never ceased to amaze him. Nicole had grown up on the other side of Tangent. He'd known her for years, thought he knew all about her. They were both products of the same culture, with family roots stretching deep down in the same sandy soil. This should have made for a happy union.

He now understood that Nicole had decided he was her best bet for escape.

Truth of the matter was that neither one of them had leveled with the other. He'd taken it for granted she understood he was a man who was doing exactly what he wanted to do. He'd ignored the signs of her restlessness, of her darting interests and longing for wild escapades. If he thought about it at all, he chalked it up to spirit, reminiscent of his mother.

By the time their differences surfaced, Nicole was pregnant. Jack suggested counseling but capitulated when she refused. And after Ginny was born, he decided he would do everything in his power to make Nicole happy and thus keep his family together.

She decided she wanted to try sculpting, so he'd built her a studio away from the house as requested. Then, at a fund-raiser for the hospital, she met an avant-garde artist gaining fame with movie stars and politicians alike, and demanded having her portrait done. He'd moved heaven and earth—to say nothing of a hefty chunk of change from savings into checking—to engage the fellow. The rest, as they say, is history. The only good thing to come from those four years was Ginny.

Lifting her down from his shoulders, he kissed his daughter's golden head. She was growing up so fast. Sometimes he had to remind himself not to hold on too tightly.

"Watch your pretty dress," he told her as her feet hit the bricks. He knew it was a stupid remark; he didn't give a damn about the dress. What he wanted to say was: *Be careful. Don't hit your head. Don't scrape your bare knees. Don't let anyone break your heart.*

She caught sight of one of her little buddies, and scooted away without a backward glance.

The door opposite him opened, and for a second, his heart leapt into his throat. *Roxanne.* But it was Sal who emerged into the courtyard, her wizened face preoccupied. When Jack smiled at her, she lowered her eyes and glanced away.

Slightly alarmed, he strode toward her, absently acknowledging greetings. "Sal?"

Reluctantly it seemed, she turned to face him.

"Sal, what's wrong?" She was pale and trembling and he reached for her wrist. His first thought was her heart. She'd had trouble the year before, even had a stint in the hospital. "Are you okay?"

"Fine, fine," she sputtered, pulling her hand away.

"But—"

"Stop playing doctor," she demanded, visually summoning her reserves. Sal Collins was a strong woman. She didn't like to be coddled, and Jack knew from a lifetime of experience, if she didn't want to talk about something, then she wouldn't. For instance, before she'd come to live with his family, she'd been married and had a baby but lost both. She'd never mentioned them to him. Not a word. Jack had only found out the year before when Sal became ill and he dug up old records.

However, she wasn't the only stubborn one living at the Wheeler ranch. "Not until you let me take your pulse."

She extended her wrist and managed a smile. "Honestly."

Her heartbeat seemed normal enough and there were color spots appearing on her cheeks as Jack's actions began to draw attention. Her skin wasn't clammy.

"People are looking," she whispered.

"Any pain in your chest? Shortness of breath? Dizziness?"

"No, no and no. Let go of me."

"Okay, but I'm keeping my eye on you," he said, leaning down to brush her forehead with a kiss.

Sal patted his cheek before withdrawing to a wooden bench. She was well liked and immediately surrounded. Only his two elderly spinster aunts kept their distance. Jack looked around to find Ginny, saw her and three other children sizing up the presents and smiled to himself.

He glanced at Sal again, relieved to see she was returning to her old self. Whatever had upset her apparently was passing. With the arrival of more guests, he devoted himself to mingling and chatting, but each time a door opened, he held his breath.

Amid the ribbing and the laughing, he found himself wondering what had happened to Roxanne.

He was visiting with one of his favorite patients and her husband when Roxanne stepped into the courtyard. For an instant he didn't hear a word of their conversation.

Nicole had loved to make an entrance, arriving in a flutter of flowing clothes, in a cloud of floral perfume, her laughter as big as she was tiny, like an exotic bird a man wanted to capture in his hands.

Tall and slender, long hair loose on her shoulders, Rox-

anne looked...well, real. Moving with the grace and ease
that were undoubtedly the by-products of good health and
regular workouts, she found her way to a quiet edge of the
garden, off to the side and not in the center. She was shy,
he realized, ill at ease amid so many strangers. Her oval
face was devoid of makeup, even lipstick. Her skin was
oddly striped with sunburn and—get this—she didn't seem
to care!

She was prettier than Nicole had ever been, he realized
with a start. Or maybe she wasn't quite as pretty. Maybe
that was it. At any rate, he couldn't take his eyes off her.

Roxanne fidgeted with the concho belt as she watched
Jack approach. For a second, when their eyes first met, she
could have sworn he'd almost looked pleased to see her,
but the moment passed so quickly, it might never have
happened.

He didn't look angry—he just looked overwhelmed. It
was a look she was coming to recognize.

"This is quite a party," she said, deciding to take the
upper hand. Ginny and a few other children wound their
way in and out between the adults, a couple of whom were
holding infants. Chatter and music competed with the soft
sound of falling water. A haze of smoke in one corner
announced the barbecue, and delicious odors permeated the
air, making Roxanne's empty stomach growl. Carl roamed
the courtyard with a tray of appetizers.

Roxanne was aware of a bevy of raised eyebrows and
wondered if Jack's friends were curious who the stranger
was. One woman in particular, the pregnant redhead Jack
had been talking to, seemed especially curious.

Roxanne wished she could make an announcement: "My
car's broken down!" she'd say. Then she could try again
with Sal.

"That's Nancy Kaufman giving you the once-over," Jack said.

"She's pretty. Pregnant, too. As a matter of fact, I see quite a few of your friends are wearing maternity smocks. Has everyone here just given birth or become pregnant?"

"Not me. Not my two elderly aunts over by the fountain, the ones waving their hankies at you."

Roxanne waved back. "You know what I mean," she said. "Grace and Nancy are pregnant, as are those three women sitting under an umbrella, and at least one of your horses. There are babies everywhere—in their father's arms, in slings, in strollers, not to mention the kittens and puppies and Goldy's foal…. It's like an epidemic."

He smiled, perhaps for the first time. It was genuine and dazzling, and Roxanne felt her throat constrict at the pure beauty of it. "They don't have babies up in Seattle?" he said, his lips still curved and so appealing.

"No. We have bypassed the whole pregnancy thing up in the great Northwest. You Southerners keep moving up, we don't need to replenish the population from our own stock."

"I've heard about you people and your regional biases," he said.

She laughed.

"Nancy is our local celebrity," he added. "She runs the radio station in Tangent."

"I interned at a radio station back in my late, great college days. I can't believe that Tangent actually has one."

"It's pretty amazing, isn't it? We have to drive almost twenty miles to a hospital, but we have a radio station. A very small one, mind you, but nevertheless…well, go figure. Anyway, I told her about you, and she said she'd like to meet a big-time television producer."

"So would I," Roxanne said.

With a lazy gaze, he added, "You look very, very nice."

"Thanks," she murmured, unsure how to return the compliment without drooling all over him. Gone was the sexy, hot cowboy with the surly brow and the impatient manner. This was the refined doctor, his brown hair glistening with health in the late-day sun, his face cleanly shaved, a soft gray shirt tucked into darker gray slacks. He smelled divine—masculine and clean, a combination of soap and desert heat. This man was just as desirable, she decided, perhaps more so.

He looked as though he had something on his mind but wasn't sure how to go about saying it.

"Ginny is an adorable little girl," Roxanne said as Sal and Grace tied a blindfold around the child's head. They twirled her around before arming her with a tail to pin on a paper donkey. Ginny was wearing a fluttery yellow dress, little golden curls kissing the back of her fragile neck. She looked sweet enough to eat with a spoon.

What a thought!

"She's a great kid," Jack said, his voice softening as it always seemed to do when he spoke about his daughter. "She can hardly wait until it's time to open the presents. Do you remember being that young?"

"I didn't have birthday parties," Roxanne said softly.

"None?"

"Well, when I got older, two girlfriends came over and we slept in my grandmother's attic. Does that count?"

"Did they bring gifts?"

"I think so."

"Then it counts."

She would have happily spent the rest of the afternoon gazing up into his eyes, but she was suddenly aware they were attracting more than a few pointed glances. She said, "Jack, I don't mean to alarm you, but everyone is staring at us."

He smiled again. Really, his smile was addictive. Did he

look at his patients like this, she wondered, as though he was memorizing their faces? She trembled inside, imagining again the feel of his touch, knowing there was no way she could ever have this man as her doctor—she was way too aware of him as a man, period. Better to stick with old Dr. Conroy back home!

Touching her arm, he murmured, "Well, you're a novelty. Here you are, a beautiful stranger talking to the scorned doctor. Heck, people are bound to be curious about you."

She was so aware of his fingers on her arm that she felt like screaming. His touch was like a hot ember—oh, crazy, crazy. Maybe it was the sunburned skin protesting even a gentle touch. Maybe that was it. But he'd said she was beautiful....

She blurted out, "I wish Oz would call."

"I'm afraid that may take a while." He seemed to notice that his fingers still rested on her forearm and withdrew his hand hastily.

"Carl said the same thing," she mumbled. "About Oz, I mean. And Sal mentioned someone named Lisa and twins who had colds."

"You talked to Sal? When?"

"A little while ago."

He frowned and glanced over at the older woman, then back at Roxanne. His eyes narrowed as he studied her face. She thought she might spontaneously combust if he didn't stop looking at her like that.

"Who is Lisa?" she squeaked.

His voice distracted, he said, "Oz's wife. Lisa is trying to take care of newborn twins by herself. Sometimes, when she gets to the end of her rope, she calls Oz to come on home, hands over the babies, takes the phone off the hook and crashes."

The faint upward curl of lips faded as he touched her

arm again, motioning her to join him in the shadows by the open door leading back into the kitchen.

For one crazy second, she thought he was going to kiss her. It didn't make any sense that he would—not in front of his friends, not at his child's birthday party, not when they barely knew each other—but she felt herself tense all the same. And she knew she wouldn't stop him if he did.

She had never felt this immediate and profound an attraction to a man before. On the other hand, she'd never crashed a car, gotten lost in the desert and been rescued by an intense, handsome, enigmatic doctor before, either. It was bound to rattle a girl's equilibrium.

Nevertheless, this attraction, unlike the logical, sensible attractions she'd experienced before, was hot and sexy and overpowering. This was hormones on alert. This reduced her to quivering Jell-O. This had her heart pounding like a jackhammer and her breath coming in little shallow gulps.

He lowered his head until his breath was actually warm against her cheek. As she anticipated the moment his lips would burn hers, he said, "Roxanne, you said a minute ago that you spoke with Sal."

Not what she expected. "Yes," she mumbled. "She's a character, isn't she?"

"She's been like a mother to me."

"She said she wiped your nose."

"She was there after my own mother died. Now she helps me with Ginny. She's been a very integral, important member of my family for as long as I can remember. She's much more than an employee, more like an aunt. She would never harm anyone."

"What exactly are you trying to say, Jack?"

"I don't want to see her get hurt."

"Of course you don't."

"You said you talked to her. When she came out here, she was so agitated I actually thought something was wrong with her heart. I think you upset her." Pinning her with his gaze, he added, "I want to know exactly what happened. What did you say to her?"

"I asked her if she knew Dolly Aames."

He rubbed his jaw impatiently. "What did she say?"

"She turned white as a sheet and said no, she'd never heard of her. One minute she was friendly and warm, and the next minute she couldn't wait to get away from me. I think she's lying. She knows something about Dolly Aames."

"If she did, she'd say so."

"Are you sure, Jack?"

"Of course. Why would she lie about something like that?"

Roxanne shook her head. "I don't know."

"She wouldn't. You must have misunderstood."

"Hardly," she said, growing increasingly brusque.

"Maybe it was the way you grilled her," he said.

"Oh, you mean when I shoved those bamboo shoots under her fingernails? Or maybe it was the anthill. What do you think? Was that over the top?"

Looking startled, he said, "I didn't mean to imply—"

Very quietly she said, "Yes, you did, Jack."

With that, she turned on her borrowed heels and left the courtyard, too angry and too embarrassed to stay another moment.

He didn't follow, thank heavens. She put a hand to her burning cheek and went right past the chilled platters of food, her appetite gone. Out the back door, across the yard now cluttered with parked cars, past the corral and the curious gazes of the horses, toward the barn—it was the only retreat she could think of.

That man!

He'd accused her of harassing an older woman!

Okay, so maybe she could have handled it better, but his

obtuse self-righteousness had irritated the living daylights out of her.

Did he really think she would repay his kindness by trying to make his valued friend so sick she appeared to be having heart problems? The thought that her innocent questions had affected Sal to that extreme made Roxanne nauseous.

It was obvious that Sal was hiding something or someone. The question now was, did Roxanne dare try to figure out what or whom?

She had never been in a situation quite like this one. She was in a strange state, wearing someone else's clothes, stuck at a stranger's home because her car had died miles from anywhere, dependent on one man whose wife was having trouble dealing with twin babies and another man who thought she was a rabble-rouser. She couldn't even use the phone and call a cab to come get her because there was no way on earth she was going back in that house.

Goldy nudged Roxanne's arm but this time, even though she hadn't been aware that she'd stopped right in front of the mare's stall, Roxanne didn't flinch. Peering inside, she found the baby curled in a long-legged bundle on the straw.

She ran a hand down Goldy's long nose, amazed at the heavy warmth of her exhaled breath and her soft, soft muzzle.

"What do I do now?" she whispered.

Aggie, the mother dog, appeared at her knees. Roxanne bent to pet the animal's sleek head. Reassured, apparently, that Roxanne wasn't there to abscond with her puppies, Aggie retreated back to the big box Carl had placed in one of the empty stalls, back to the excited yips of her brood.

Roxanne peeked outside and was relieved to find that no one was searching for her. She didn't want Jack leaving his daughter's birthday party to come looking for her.

Did she?

Absolutely not. She never wanted to see that man again, period.

By the looks of the amount of food Grace had prepared, Roxanne figured she was in for a long wait. She formulated a plan as she wandered back into the barn, coming to a rest by the stack of bales. Once people started leaving, it would be easy enough to find a ride into Tangent. All she needed to do was wait out the party.

Unbidden, the seductive memory of Jack's face lowering to hers came stampeding back. She recalled the masculine scent of his skin and the certainty she'd had that he was going to kiss her. It had seemed so right, regardless of the other people around. Her lips had trembled with anticipation.

And then there was Ginny, a little princess in buttery yellow. Roxanne felt a stab of regret that she would miss seeing Ginny open her presents. What had Jack put in the pink box with the pink bow? She'd looked forward to finding out.

Oh, well. These people were strangers. Most likely she'd never see any of them again.

She was suddenly itching to get back to work. Seeking comfort on familiar ground, she thought about her upcoming schedule. The boss wanted her to showcase local entrepreneurs. Roxanne wasn't thrilled with the prospect of lining up one wealthy hotshot after the other, but the ratings showed viewers loved it. And ratings were everything in television. After that, the powers that be wanted her to concentrate on lottery winners, game show winners and other windfall millionaires. Nouveau riche was big this year.

She felt a wave of irritation rise in her throat when she thought about her own idea, formulated on the long drive down here and dismissed over the phone by the general manager, Leon Mackey. "Not enough glitz," he'd said.

"It's been done before." And her favorite: "No one cares about this kind of stuff, Roxanne."

No one cares about local heroes, about people risking themselves to make the world safer or better? Was that really true? Was everyone really that cynical?

She refused to believe it. When she got back she would just have to push harder. She'd have to dig for the right angle to combine the stories she was dying to tell with the station's need to sell commercial time. She wanted to tell stories about people. Real people. People who made a difference. People who needed people. The song refrain filled her head.

Roxanne patted Aggie again, taking a moment to touch each plump puppy, then climbed up into the hay, settling at last near the crevice that held the cat family. Mother and kittens were asleep.

She, of course, was way too riddled with anxiety to sleep. She had to listen for cars, for voices, for anything that would signal a possible ride into town. She cradled her head against her folded arms and steadfastly worked at expunging any lingering thoughts of sultry blue eyes. Of crushed hats and broad shoulders. Of strong arms she ached to have enfold her. Of shy smiles that pierced her heart.

No! She would not think about Jack Wheeler.

She shuddered, suddenly cold for no reason. It was warm outside, but she shivered again.

She thought of the flowers, the fountain, the kittens. She thought of Ginny's flaxen curls and a baby horse someone should give a name. Sunny, maybe. Or Marmalade. She filled her mind with synonyms for yellow. Gradually her tumultuous thoughts receded as the barn and its inhabitants settled into the evening with a soft sigh.

Chapter Four

It took some doing, but for the rest of the party Jack managed to sidestep questions about Roxanne. Everyone there had seen what turned out to be the ill-advised tête-à-tête in the corner and were bursting with curiosity. Who was the tall blonde? Where did she run off to? What was going on?

He shook his head a lot, looked bewildered—which wasn't a difficult expression to assume—and got on with the business of hosting a birthday party. He took oodles of pictures, cuddled plump little babies he'd delivered himself, held Ginny as she blew out her three pink candles and smiled as she smeared chocolate cake from one end of her party dress to the other.

But in the back of his mind, playing and replaying, was a tape of the conversation he'd had with Roxanne. In his memory it didn't seem to him that he'd been all that reprehensible. He'd just wanted a few answers. He was just trying to protect his home turf from the appealing interloper.

Was that the whole truth? Looking back, he could see

that he'd wanted to be angry with her. When she'd cracked the door a little, he barreled his way through, doing whatever he could to make her mad, to make her less desirable, to make her leave.

He'd succeeded. It was the most hollow victory he'd ever won, but it was necessary; he knew that.

It was a relief when people started leaving, when Sal insisted Ginny was so wired from all the sweets and excitement that she needed a calming bath. Grace said she would do it, but she looked exhausted. As her physician and her employer, he ordered her to bed, waving aside Carl's offers of help.

Sal bathed Ginny and Carl looked after Grace, so Jack did his best to move the leftovers into the refrigerator. He wanted to leave it to rot—he wanted to go find Roxanne. He was angry with her and worried about her at the same time, warring emotions that made his gut hurt.

As he worked, he formulated a plan. He would insist Roxanne accept a ride back into town. He'd take her to her car where she could retrieve her suitcases. Then they'd go on to the motel. Sal wasn't up to a meddlesome female, and come to think of it, neither was he.

Sadie and Veronica, Jack's elderly aunts, and their geriatric driver, George, feigned assistance with the dishes while doing their best to pump him for information about Roxanne. Eventually they gave up, kissed him on his cheek and went home.

With the food put away and the dishes stacked next to the sink, he looked in on Ginny. She was tucked under a quilt Jack's mother had made many years before, her eyes closed, her breathing even. He wondered if his mother had ever once contemplated the fact that her quilt would someday cover her granddaughter, a child she'd never meet. Sal, in a chair beside the bed, had nodded off, as well. Rousing her, he sent her to bed, then leaned down and kissed his birthday girl, reveling in the just-bathed scent of her pink skin and shiny hair.

"Happy birthday, sweetpea," he whispered as he turned off the light and half closed the door.

It crossed his mind that with Grace pregnant and Sal looking peaked, he'd better start looking around for additional domestic help.

At last the house was quiet.

At last it was time to find Roxanne…but where?

Knowing she wasn't stupid enough to head back out into the desert, that left the house, the barn and the distant bungalow to search. Since she'd never even seen the bungalow, it seemed unlikely she'd be drinking beer and watching satellite television with the hired hands. He'd already searched the house, so that left the barn.

He gathered his truck keys, a bottle of cold water and the aspirin, then walked on out into the night. The moon was waxing—it would be full in a few days—but it still packed enough wattage to bathe the yard in its shimmery yellow glow. For once the huge sky overhead failed to soothe him. Even the lone cry of a distant coyote resonated the melancholy he could feel building in his heart.

As he passed the two corralled horses, they whinnied. The pale mare appeared at the split rails, and Milo, the larger bay gelding was a shifting shape behind her. Jack could hear hoofs beat the dirt as the mare paraded around the edge of the fence, sure he'd come to offer a nighttime treat like he usually did.

"Sorry, girl, no carrots tonight," he said.

His confidence that Roxanne had retreated to the barn began to ebb as it dawned on him the place was pitch-black. It was hard to picture a city slicker like Roxanne sitting in the dark with animals all around her. He nudged the big door open with his foot and with the bottom of the water bottle flicked on just one modest light.

Goldy looked at him with liquid-brown eyes. He paused long enough to mutter a few soothing words to the new mama and to admire her offspring, then he headed toward the stack of hay, Aggie's puppies yipping as he passed. Sure enough, he found Roxanne perched halfway up, head reclined on folded arms. She appeared to be sound asleep.

He paused for a moment, relieved beyond reason that she was still here and hadn't done something rash and impetuous like striking out on her own. That's when he noticed her skirt was caught, exposing a long stretch of naked, creamy thigh, the hint of black lace up near the curve of her bottom.

"Holy cow," he whispered, clearing his throat. As she stirred, he fought the urge to dash out of the barn. He watched in tense silence as she stretched, shuddered, twisted her head and met his gaze.

Lord, was she beautiful. Her hair was in disarray, splayed across her flushed cheek and shoulders, her eyes vivid despite the poor light. In an instant, he thought that this was how she would look to a lover, to a man welcome in her bed and in her life. He felt deep stirrings all throughout his body and an ache that he would never know her in that way.

The black dress was covered with straw, a few pieces of which clung to her hair and to her face, neck and arms. They gave her an innocent look at odds with the temptress staring at him through dark, mysterious eyes.

He tried a smile. As it got little or no response from her, he figured it hadn't come out so good, so he cleared his throat again—there suddenly seemed to be a bevy of frogs lodged in his windpipe—and spoke.

"I've come to...well, make sure you're all right," he said as he started climbing, his gaze on her face instead of on her leg, stopping when he was one bale below hers. With him standing and her sitting, he had the advantage of looking down at her.

Behind her, the kittens mewed for their mother who appeared from the top of the pile and jumped down next to them. The cries got frantic, then a peaceful silence resumed.

Roxanne sighed so deeply, her breasts swelled against the taut fabric of her dress and Jack almost fell over backward. "Doesn't their life seem…well, unfettered?" she whispered, bending her golden head to look down at the cats.

"Well, actually, the mother cat was abandoned near my clinic. You should have seen her. All skin and bones and a bulging middle."

"That's not what I mean."

He watched the cats for a second and mumbled, "It does seem like they've got things down to basics."

"Why can't life be that easy for people?"

"Yeah," he said idly.

"No, I mean it," she said, her voice thoughtful.

He felt a little lost. He'd expected recriminations from her, accusations, protestations. He hadn't expected a philosophical discourse on cats versus human beings. He said, "I'm not so sure it isn't, Roxanne."

"No, it's not," she said. "People have to make choices."

"I think cats have to make choices, too, don't you?"

Her head lifted and she turned the full force of her gaze on him. The impact was like a slap. "No," she said vehemently, "it's not the same. Cats run on instincts. If they do make choices, it's whether to sit out in the sun or under a bush, catch a mouse or snag a bird, turn right or turn left. People have to make choices. Cats just…well, do things."

"Do things," he repeated.

"Yes."

"Like…making a nest in the straw?"

"And filling it with babies," she mumbled, her eyelashes fluttering in a beguiling and rather touching way. "Things like that."

She looked so vulnerable he wanted to hug her. But her words had awakened other thoughts, as well. Her ruminations reminded him of Nicole who had been a combination of woman and cat, he thought suddenly. Nicole, running on instinct, ultimately making choices, some of them dreadful, some of them with consequences for an innocent like Ginny.

Caught in his own unhappy thoughts, he jumped when Roxanne spoke again. "Is that water?"

He glanced at her just in time to see the tip of a pink tongue flick across her lips. Swallowing hard, he mumbled, "I'm always pushing water."

"And I never turn it down," she said as she took the proffered bottle, screwed off the lid and drank.

He was trying hard not to stare at her, but it was damn near impossible. If push came to shove, he knew he couldn't explain why Roxanne Salyer had him in such a knot. Why her, and not the dozens of other good-looking, pleasant, unencumbered local women? How many of them, after Nicole went her merry way, made it real clear they considered him a good catch?

Now this woman, who seemed as much child as adult, had his insides churning just because she ran her tongue over her lips, just because a glimpse of her underwear had his imagination running on overtime. For heaven's sake, he was a thirty-nine-year-old man! He growled, "How do you feel?"

"Fine."

"Sure you do."

"Okay, not very good. There. Does that make you happy?"

"No, not particularly."

Her eyes widened and she stood. "What time is it?"

He reached out to steady her. His touch on her arm elicited a sharp intake of her breath. He'd forgotten all about the sunburn.

"I need to catch a ride," she said, looking at his hand, which he hastily withdrew. "I can't believe I fell asleep."

"You were going to leave without telling me?"

"What do you care where I go or what I do?"

"I don't," he replied gruffly.

"Besides, I would think you'd be very glad to see me go."

"Not like that," he grumbled. "Not just disappearing. Anyway, everyone's gone."

"Then I'll walk," she said. But as she said it, she sank back down onto the bale of straw. Her eyes were glittery and he suspected she was trying not to cry.

Damn, he mumbled deep inside. He was a sucker for tears. They could be newborn, maudlin, pouty, grief-stricken, happy or manipulative—it didn't matter. One glimpse of a tear and he was a goner. He steeled himself and added, "You can't walk."

"Don't tell me what I can or can't do," she snapped. "I'm twenty-seven years old. Besides, I know the way now. I can spend the night in my car."

This was so absurd, he had to fight the urge to laugh. "Well, watch out for the coyotes and the snakes."

"There are no coyotes—" she said, but right on cue, a muffled but distinct coyote call echoed outside, and her eyes grew wide with alarm.

"I'll drive you," he said. Then he took a really good look at her and felt his resolution falter. "You're sick."

"No—"

He touched her forehead with the back of his hand and cursed, again, deep down inside where she couldn't hear. "You're running a slight fever."

"It's the sunburn."

"Yes, it's the sunburn. You're having chills, aren't you, and a headache? I bet your skin feels like it shrank, like it doesn't fit anymore. Am I right?"

"So now you're a mind reader?"

"No, just a doctor." He shook out a couple of aspirin, which she dutifully swallowed. They stared at each other for a few seconds.

Finally she said, "I shouldn't have walked out on you, not in the middle of your daughter's party. You just made me so angry."

"I gathered that. But you have to understand that Sal is like family to me."

She nodded as she shifted her gaze away from his.

"I just want you to leave her alone."

"There you go again, making it sound like I plan to beat her up. I asked her a few questions, Jack. That's all. She's hiding something."

"Whatever," he told her. She was so damn stubborn!

"Within the hour, I'll be tucked away in Tangent," she said. "Sal's secrets will be safe."

"You won't be in Tangent," he said firmly.

This earned him a raised pair of nicely shaped eyebrows.

"You're sick," he added.

"Not that sick."

"Still, I'd feel better if you were close by until the worst of this is over. I'll drive you into town tomorrow when I go check up on the twins. Oz will be there so you can finally talk to him about your car. Really, Roxanne, this is best."

"I can't."

"Why not?"

For the count of ten she said nothing. Then her gaze shifted again and she whispered, "I've already been such a bother."

He tilted her chin gently until she was looking up at him again. Her eyes were velvet pools, dark and deep, and damned if he didn't sense an invitation lurking in the warm depths. He fought the gravitational pull, his mouth to hers, his body to hers—he fought the urge to kiss her, to ravage her, to burn her right out of his system.

"You haven't been a burden," he said, amazed at how sincere his voice sounded, how casual, how blasé—how normal. "Come inside," he added softly. "Have something to eat. You must be starving. Then you can have a cool bath and go to bed. Is this advice really so hard to take?"

Again she stared at him, then she shook her head.

"Good. Come on."

He took her hand and helped her down to the wooden floor, releasing her as soon as possible because he didn't trust himself. Again they stared at each other. It was awkward and arousing at the same time. He loved the chestnut depths of her eyes, her thick lashes, the challenge he perceived in her expression.

Out of the corner of his eye, he saw Goldy give him the once-over, her demeanor calm, her foal asleep in the shadows.

As they left the barn, it seemed to Jack like his horse smirked at him.

Roxanne lowered her body into a cool bath and alternately shivered and sighed. Jack had given her something soothing to dump into the water and it felt heavenly. A couple of leftover sandwiches had taken care of her empty stomach, and now she directed her efforts toward relaxing.

She closed her eyes and tried to summon a peaceful scene, like Puget Sound on a calm day, the deep water as blue as...Jack's eyes.

No! She would not think about Jack.

So, back to restful images. The trees. Thousands of evergreens. Stands of fir and pine, all as tall and strong as...Jack.

This wasn't working. After several more moments of fruitless daydreaming, she gave up. She was restless and yet spent, distracted in a totally new way.

And, surprise, surprise, it was all because of Jack.

Looking down at him as he climbed those bales in the barn, his gaze riveted to her face, his muscular body moving resolutely toward her, his lips parted slightly, his demeanor so, so...focused—it had been all she could do to remember two things. One: breathe in, breathe out. Two: she was *very* angry with him.

And now, because he'd been charming and sweet and so persistent, she was in his bathroom, soaking in his tub, about to lie down in his bed because he wanted her in the one room with an air conditioner. He was treating her politely and with kindness.

And she wanted more.

Well, of course she did, she rationalized as she got out of the tub and carefully towel-dried her tender skin. She wanted to know about Dolly. She wanted to be able to return home to her grandmother with some kind of information. She wanted a lead about where Dolly may have gone.

It all had nothing to do with Jack. Nothing to do with his eyes. Nothing to do with the way he used those eyes to delve right into her. Nothing to do with the way he moved or talked or sighed. Nothing with the heat of his body as he stood over her or the feel of his hand on her forehead or the sight of him putting together a makeshift meal for her in his kitchen.

Nope. It was just that he was acting like a very strong, very enticing roadblock.

Roadblocks, however, were made to be circumvented. It was imperative she keep her eye on the larger picture. She needed to find Dolly Aames for Grandma Nell—and relatively soon, too. Grandma needed something to look forward to.

Her grandmother had had breast cancer the year before and now iffy test results and a bothersome cough had everyone worried about a relapse. In fact, Roxanne realized, the older woman was due for a chest X ray on Wednesday.

It wasn't as though Grandma Nell was alone. Roxanne's mother had hired a retired neighbor, Linda Wills, to stay with her, but Roxanne felt uneasy being so far away. "I'll call tomorrow," she said aloud, and immediately felt a little better. Maybe by then she'd have news about Dolly—if she could get Sal alone again....

Roxanne pulled a thin cotton gown over her head and wondered if it was another loan from Grace or something left by Jack's ex-wife when she ran off with her lover. Again she shook her head in disbelief. What kind of idiot gave up this wonderful home, to say nothing of a man like Jack? What kind of blithering fool sacrificed a precious little girl like Ginny?

Maybe the woman didn't like babies, she thought suddenly. Maybe she wasn't the nurturing type.

Am I the nurturing type...? she wondered.

This internal dialogue wasn't going anywhere. Roxanne walked around the big bedroom, absorbing details of Jack's life. There was a large studio portrait of Ginny on one side of the tall chest of drawers, and a photograph of Jack, Ginny and Sal all on horseback on the other. Roxanne picked up this picture—she recognized the horses from the corral. Sal sat atop Sprite, her hair as white as the horse's coat. Jack was on Milo, Ginny perched in the saddle in front of him, both their faces split into huge grins. Roxanne smiled back at them.

She opened and sniffed bottles of manly fragrances that all looked untouched—undoubtedly gifts he didn't use. She admired the framed Diego Rivera print of a lily vendor, sat on the edge of the white coverlet, studied the pattern of brick tiles that composed the floor. Cool air hissed from a window air conditioner, lifting her bangs.

It was no good; she could not rest in that room. It was too…Jack.

Looking around, she found what had to be his lightweight robe tossed across the back of a chair, and put it on over the gown. She opened the door carefully, anxious not to wake anyone.

The door to the room across from hers was ajar, and being naturally nosy, she peeked inside. It was a child's room, all pink and frilly, with white furniture, mounds of stuffed animals, shelves of books—a little girl's haven. Ginny was asleep on her back, most of her covers kicked off, a fan overhead stirring the air, her golden hair spread across the pillow.

For several moments, Roxanne stood in the darkened hallway and stared at the child. She listened to the sound of Ginny's breathing, so regular and peaceful, and she realized that Ginny was like a treasure, kept safe in her father's home, in her father's heart. The thought made her feel like crying.

Why was she suddenly so emotional? This wasn't like her. She was a steely career woman.

Eventually she tiptoed away. She found the kitchen without much effort and immediately felt renewed pangs of hunger. There were stacks of dishes by the sink and she stared at them for several seconds while her mind raced.

The trouble was she was becoming too indebted to Jack Wheeler. She was staying in his house, eating his food, taking his aspirin, depending on him to drive her around. It not only robbed her of her independence, but it made her accountable to him, and she didn't like the feeling. Besides, if she was going to pursue her plan to find out about Dolly, she couldn't necessarily play by his rules.

She had a feeling he wouldn't accept money from her as recompense, but she could wash the party dishes, and that would make her feel as though she'd done something to even the score. She rolled up her sleeves, found rubber gloves under the sink to protect her sunburned hands and arms and commenced washing.

It took well over three hours to wash and dry and find homes for the dozens and dozens of plates, platters, bowls and glasses, and what seemed like hundreds of pieces of silverware. She had a feeling Grace would spend the next month trying to find things. Mostly it took so long because Roxanne tried so hard to be quiet. When she was done, she opened the refrigerator and perused the interior, hesitating over the leftover barbecued chicken, settling on the bowl of melon balls.

Stabbing a couple with a fork, she wandered into the living room, a place she hadn't been before. It was a masculine room—like the rest of the house, except for Ginny's little corner. She wondered if Jack had obliterated any trace of his wife after she left or if the woman had moved like a ghost through the house, leaving no imprint anywhere. She munched on watermelon as her attention was captured by a tank of fish that seemed to contain two big gray ones and dozens of babies.

What was it about this place and babies?

She thought about settling down in the dark green rocker or curling up in the brown leather chair, but decided against it. Pulling a book by one of her favorite authors off the shelf, she returned the fork to the kitchen, then made her way back to Jack's bedroom, past several closed doors, wondering behind which he slumbered, kicked out of his bedroom by a sunburned pain in the neck.

As she fell at last into bed, the cool sheets like ambrosia

against her skin, she thought to herself that washing a few dishes wasn't nearly enough to settle her debt. She'd have to think of something else.

Roxanne woke the next morning with a start. She sat up quickly, looked out the window, glanced at the clock. It was before six o'clock. She'd always been an early riser. If she were at home in Seattle, she'd put on her running shoes and jog for a couple of miles before showering and dressing for work, but here she was stuck with the black dress and sandals. No jogging.

Today—come what may—she was recovering the suitcases from her dead car.

She got up and slipped on Jack's robe again, twisted her mop of sleep-bent hair up but let it fall when she realized she didn't have anything with which to clip it in place. She borrowed Jack's comb to tug at the tangles, then after looking in Ginny's room and admiring the still-sleeping child, made her way to the kitchen.

Lucky day! The room was empty except for the morning sun and Sal, seated at the counter on a stool, a mug and an open paperback book in front of her. Her white hair was damp as though she'd just showered. This morning she was wearing a faded denim shirt with a high collar, and red-framed reading glasses. When she looked up, the warm smile of greeting faded right off her lips.

Roxanne gestured at the mug. "Is there more where that came from?"

Sal blinked a couple of times and jumped off her stool. For a minute or so, she busied herself readying Roxanne's coffee. Roxanne had meant to get it herself, but it was obvious Sal needed this time to get used to the idea that Roxanne was in the kitchen and not gone.

Roxanne took a stool across from Sal and sat down. She

read the author's upside-down name and commented, "I like this guy, too."

Sal closed the book as she handed Roxanne the mug. "I don't," she said.

All righty! Roxanne thanked Sal for the coffee and took a sip. "This is delicious."

Sal remained standing.

"I think that perhaps Seattle is at least partly responsible for the coffee craze that's sweeping the nation."

No response.

"Leave it to us to take a fifty-cent cup of joe from the diner and turn it into a five-dollar latte at an espresso bar."

Sal, gripping the back of her stool with both hands, leaned forward slightly and said, "Why are you here?"

Cut to the chase, huh? Roxanne said, "I told you, I'm looking for an old friend of my grandmother's, Dolly Aames."

"Are you having any luck?"

"So far, my best lead is your unwillingness to answer me."

Sal blinked.

"Maybe it's the name that's throwing you. Dolly would have been about your height, maybe a tad taller. She had blue eyes like yours, a distinctive mole on the right side of her neck and long reddish hair. Grandma described her as a 'dreamy flirt.'"

Sal shook her head.

"I just want to find her to ease my grandmother's mind," Roxanne added.

"Ease her mind?"

"They were friends."

"Friends," Sal said.

"Yes."

"Is your grandmother okay?"

Roxanne hadn't planned to reveal any details, but she

sensed that if she wanted the truth from Sal, then she'd better deliver it herself. She said, "Gran was sick last year. Really sick."

"But she's better now and wants to find this old friend of hers?"

Roxanne managed to say, "Yes, very much." Was her grandmother better or in the midst of a decline? She didn't know—that was the problem.

Sal said, "I wish I could help you, but I can't."

Roxanne had been so sure Sal was about to reveal something. A disappointed "But—" escaped her lips.

"Besides, what I meant was, why are you here, in this house? I thought you left yesterday during the party."

"Jack insisted I stay," Roxanne said.

"Where?"

"In his bedroom."

Sal's new, friendlier persona was gone in a flash. "What!"

"No, no that's not what I mean. You don't understand—"

"It's you who doesn't understand! How dare you sashay around in Jack's robe!"

"What the heck do you mean by that crack?"

"You know darn well what I mean."

"Do you honestly think I'd sleep with Jack when Ginny is right across the hall?"

From the doorway came a very masculine voice. "Morning, ladies."

Both women turned.

From the gleam in his eyes, it seemed obvious he'd heard at least a little of the exchange, and Roxanne felt like slinking into a hole.

"Shame on you, Sal, for thinking such things," Jack said, patting her shoulder.

Sal laughed.

Jack turned his attention next to Roxanne. He was imposing in beat-up leather boots and jeans that, though worn, conformed to his muscular legs in a way that filled Roxanne with out-and-out lust. He looked like a man who took what he wanted from life.

That was a little fanciful, she admitted, the by-product, perhaps, of watching too many old Westerns on late-night television. But he did look capable and determined and as though he was about to swing himself into a saddle and mosey off toward the sunset, doctor's bag firmly in hand. She suddenly wished she knew how to ride so she could go with him. If that's where he was really going, and if he would want her along even if it was.

"Sal, you shouldn't have washed all those dishes," Jack said as he moved toward the coffeepot.

"I didn't," she said. "I thought you did."

"Not me. Grace must have been restless—"

"I washed the dishes," Roxanne said, surreptitiously glancing at Jack's rear. Those jeans worked wonders on every part of his anatomy.

"You?"

This was said in unison by both of them and it annoyed Roxanne. She mumbled, "Just because I don't know anything about ranching doesn't mean I can't scrub a pot."

Jack laughed, but Sal managed to look even more annoyed—no easy feat.

He said, "You must have gotten up at dawn."

"I couldn't sleep," she said, hoping that the reason she couldn't sleep—her increasingly sensual thoughts of Jack—didn't show on her face.

"Well...thanks," he said, and then turning once again to Sal, he added, "Roxanne's sunburn was bad enough that I didn't want her off somewhere by herself so I put her in my room with the air conditioner. I slept in my study. Okay?"

As an answer, Sal leaned around the counter, glanced at Roxanne's legs and said, "She looks okay now."

"Yes," Jack said, cradling his mug, looking into Roxanne's eyes for a second before his gaze drifted down to her chest. She resisted the urge to see if his robe gaped open on her and if it did, what it revealed. Did he have any idea how he affected her, she wondered? If he did, would he run for the hills, horse or no horse?

"I feel just fine," she said.

"Good. I bet you're anxious to go get your car."

Obviously he was hustling her out of his house before she could further "grill" Sal, whom he treated with such respect it was obvious their relationship had escalated from simple employer/employee a long time ago. The perverse part of her nature made her want to hang around the house with Sal. That would not only be incredibly rude to suggest, but judging from Sal's closed expression, totally pointless.

She wanted to tell Sal that this wasn't over. She wasn't a news producer for nothing. Her nose was twitching—she could smell a secret a mile away. Normally she didn't pry into things that didn't concern her, but this was different—this was for Grandma Nell. This was for…hope. Something to look forward to. Something to pull Gran through the tests and the waiting.

"Okay," she said.

Sal looked distinctly relieved.

Jack said, "Good. We'll go after I exercise the horses. Sal, why don't you come help me?"

Sal slipped out the back door as Roxanne drummed her fingers on the counter.

"Don't be too relieved, Sal. You and I will talk again," Roxanne mumbled as the door closed behind them.

Chapter Five

The morning passed with amazing speed. First Grace showed up, full of apologies for dishes left undone, stunned speechless when she discovered they'd been taken care of. Carl came next. It was Sunday, he announced, and so he and Grace were taking the day off to go on a picnic. Grace looked too tired to picnic, but she rallied at Carl's enthusiasm.

Roxanne watched them thoughtfully. She tried to think if she'd ever been around a married couple who looked out for one another like these two did. She didn't think so. Certainly not her parents, whose relationship with each other had never seemed selfless or tender, but advantageous to their individual goals.

Wasn't that what Kevin said about her? Didn't that describe every relationship she'd had since college?

The thought of her career and her ambitions made Roxanne uncomfortable. She put them out of her mind. Plenty of time to worry about her future at the station on the long drive back to Seattle.

Soon after, Ginny walked into the kitchen, announcing that she was hungry—now! As Carl and Grace were drinking coffee and juice, Roxanne found the cereal and milk. After breakfast, while Carl packed leftovers for their picnic and Grace rested with her feet up, Roxanne helped Ginny dress.

"I like pink," the child announced.

"No kidding," Roxanne said. The open drawer revealed stacks of pink shorts, pink jeans, pink socks, pink underpants and pink shirts.

Once Ginny was dressed, she wanted to visit all the animals, so Roxanne went with her. They fed carrots to the horses, dog biscuits to Aggie, cheese cubes to the mother cat and apples to the few cows lurking in a back pen.

Roxanne was very aware of Jack as he moved around the big yard, the new foal following him like a big yellow puppy. Goldy ambled along, as well, and the sight of the man and his entourage made Roxanne smile. He was so at ease outdoors, so terribly masculine. His voice could be heard soothing, coaxing, cajoling. She was so aware of him, that many times she lost track of what Ginny was saying and had to play catch-up to keep in the conversation.

Every time she caught her gaze drifting to Jack, she noticed that he seemed oblivious of her presence, which was good, wasn't it?

Then why did it make her feel sad?

After exercising the horses, Jack and Sal fed and watered the animals. As Ginny ran to help, Jack turned a fine spray of the hose on her and sprinkled her face. The child laughed and ran away, reappearing within seconds with Aggie's water dish, which she dumped on his boots. He play-acted alarm as he dropped the hose and hefted Ginny upside down onto the top of his shoulders. She was laughing so hard she couldn't talk.

It was all so normal. It all looked like such...fun.

Eventually Jack disappeared. When he showed up again, he'd changed out of his disreputable and terribly sexy jeans, metamorphosing once again into the very picture of country chic. It was amazing to Roxanne how, with the change of clothes or hats, he could transform himself from derelict cowboy to gentleman rancher to town doctor.

Sal took charge of a protesting Ginny as Jack walked into a garage and backed out a dusty silver sedan. As Roxanne climbed in, she noticed a car seat and several toys in the back seat. This was obviously the family car.

"I want to go with you," Ginny said as Jack rolled down his window to kiss her goodbye.

"Not this time, sweetpea."

"But, Daddy—"

"I'll bring you a surprise," he said.

Ginny grinned, Sal looked as though she wanted to scold him, and they left.

This newer vehicle didn't jostle its passengers with the same intensity of the old truck. It was roomier, plusher, smoother, but ironically Roxanne found herself missing the informal snugness of the truck cab.

At least her sunburn was better than it had been the day before even though the rayon dress rubbing against her knees was uncomfortable. She could hardly wait to see the last of Grace's black dress.

What bothered her more than the sunburn was the man sitting next to her, seemingly caught up in his own thoughts. She tried thinking about something besides him, but it was as though her mind had one figurative foot stuck in cement and all she could do was run around in circles.

Hence thoughts of Ginny eating her breakfast became reflections upon how the child's eyes were the spitting image of her father's. Thoughts of Grace and Carl interacting became curiosity about how Jack and his ex-wife had gotten along before things went bad. Thoughts of the baby animals reminded her of Jack's tenderness. She'd never known a man so centered on life.

She'd also never known one as gentle. Or, when it came to what he thought of as "safekeeping" his extended family, one more obstinate.

They resumed traveling after Jack retrieved Roxanne's suitcases from the trunk of her car. As the arid and seldom-changing scenery passed by her window, she said, "Jack, may I ask you a question that's none of my business?"

"Isn't that your specialty?" he quipped.

His sarcasm was unexpected, and she winced.

He looked at her, his smile paling. "I guess that wasn't as funny as I meant it to be, was it?"

"No."

"I'm sorry. Go ahead, ask me a question."

"What was in the pink box?"

"What pink box?"

"The one you had in your truck yesterday. The one with the pink bow."

"Ginny's present? Oh, that's right, you missed the present opening, didn't you?"

He cast her another half smile as though musing over the memory of their disagreement of the day before. It occurred to her that he was in a great mood—was it because he was finally getting rid of her?

"It was just a little jewelry box," he continued. "The kind with a rotating ballerina inside. A tune plays when it's opened. Ginny saw it at the general store last month."

Roxanne smiled. "I had one of those when I was a little kid," she said in one of those moments when a forgotten memory floods back. "It played 'Edelweiss.'"

"Did your dad get it for you?"

"I don't remember where it came from. I doubt it was from my father, though. He didn't have time for things like that. He was always busy making money—he still is. He's almost retired now, but he's taken up Internet trading and is doing quite well. He and Mom still live in Seattle, but they just bought a condo in New York.''

''Sounds ritzy.''

''Apparently it's quite something. It's close to Wall Street and jazz clubs for him and the theater and fancy restaurants for her. Mom loves to travel. In the last six months, she's been to Milan, Greenland and Paris. They're both tan and fit and look like an ad for some kind of midlife vitamins.''

''People often go through a period of self-improvement if not downright self-indulgence once their family responsibilities lessen,'' he said as he turned onto the main highway. There wasn't another car in sight.

''My parents have always been exactly like this,'' she said. ''When she's not jetting around, Mom is as focused on her work in real estate as Dad is on his stocks and portfolios. They both like money. They always have.''

''Do you have brothers or sisters?''

''Nope. I have Grandma Nell.'' The ache in her heart as she said this startled her. For the first time, she realized she might not always have this generous, kind, nurturing mother figure in her life. What would the world be like without Grandma Nell?

Cold. Lonely.

What if the X ray showed a shadow in her lungs?

Her mind shied away from the thought, but it came back.

A shadow would mean the disease was back. While it wouldn't be the end of all hope, it would be a step back both physically and emotionally for Grandma Nell. And for Roxanne, she admitted. Her determination to regroup The Sunflowers hardened.

''Me, neither,'' Jack said.

Roxanne had been so caught up in her anxieties, that for a second she had no idea what he was talking about.

"Dad always said they wanted more kids after me, but Mom wanted to wait a while, and then she died and 'a while' never came."

"I'm sorry," Roxanne whispered. "How did she die?"

"Her horse bolted when it came across a snake. Then the poor thing stumbled in a ravine and threw Mom to the ground. She hit her head on some rocks. It was up on that butte over there. Dad said that at least she died doing something she loved. I don't think he ever got over the fact that he couldn't save her."

"He must have loved her very much."

"Yes, he did. Anyway, after Mom died, Sal stepped in. She'd been around for most of my life, but as a housekeeper. I don't know how I would have survived my mother's death if it hadn't been for Sal."

"We both owe a lot to women who took care of us when our mothers couldn't, or wouldn't, don't we?" Roxanne said.

"Yes." He spared her a quick glance and added, "Forgive me, but your mother sounds just like my ex-wife. She didn't want a child, either. Why do women like that have children?"

"I don't know," Roxanne said, though she didn't think he was really asking her opinion. She heard pure puzzlement in his voice—hadn't she wondered the same thing?

"Tell me about your grandmother. Didn't you say she was once a singer?"

"Yes. She was a little older than the other three women in the group. Dolly was the youngest by about eight years. Maybe they were close because of their age difference. Apparently Dolly was boy crazy but could sing like an angel."

"So your grandmother acted as a sort of big sister?"

"More or less. Grandma already had my mother so she was like an old married lady to the younger women. After Dolly left without saying a word, the group more or less fell apart. They all keep in touch, however. All except Dolly.''

''Your grandmother sounds like a nice woman.''

''My grandmother is a wonderful woman,'' Roxanne said. Letting down her guard, she added, ''She had breast cancer last year. Oh, she's in remission now, but...well, lately she's been tired and her blood work looks bad and then there's this cough.... They're taking an X ray on Wednesday.''

He nodded, but didn't say anything.

''Does that sound reasonable to you? I mean, you're a doctor.''

''I assume she has a good oncologist?''

''The best.''

''Then it sounds reasonable. You should have the results very soon.''

''Yes.''

''Waiting is awful,'' he said, sparing her a quick glance. ''Especially when it's someone you love.''

''I don't know how my mother could have come from Gran,'' Roxanne added. ''They're so different.''

''Mothers and daughters often are,'' he said.

''Really?''

He cast her a perplexed glance and shrugged, as though unsure, if push came to shove, whether he believed what he was saying or not.

Roxanne hoped it was true, but she wasn't sure how a person really knew until it was too late. Again she heard Kevin's voice. *You're just like your mother.*

''What about you, Roxanne?'' Jack asked suddenly.

''What about me?''

''Well, you're a very attractive woman. Is there a steady boyfriend?''

Was he a mind reader? Startled by his timing, she mumbled, ''Not anymore.''

"But there was?"

"Yes."

"And you decided he wasn't the one."

"What does that mean?" Roxanne said, trying desperately to deflect the conversation away from Kevin, who had dumped *her,* not the other way around.

"The one. You know, the one you wanted to settle down with, build a family with."

"You're assuming I want to settle down and build a family."

"Yes."

"Why? I have a good job with excellent growth potential. I may not be in charge now, but I will be someday. Women don't define themselves anymore by having a man or a baby."

"I just thought—"

"You just assumed," she said. She knew she sounded surly and was at a loss to explain it. "You don't really know a thing about me," she added, and was chagrined to notice a tone of petulance in her voice.

"That's true," he said. "I guess I've just been watching you around Ginny and the animals."

Roxanne didn't ask what he meant. She was surprised he'd been watching her, ashamed at her outburst. He'd been nothing but kind to her—well, mostly. For twenty-seven years, she'd had herself under strict control, and now she was a blubbering fool who couldn't sleep, who couldn't even hold her temper.

It's Grandma Nell, she told herself. *I'm worried sick about her. I'm afraid for her. I'm afraid for me.* She tried to think of some way to recapture their ease with one another and came up empty.

"There's Nancy Kaufman's radio station," he said as they passed a narrow dirt road leading to a small adobe building complete with a tall radio tower and a huge tree out front. A sign dangling from a post said simply KGAL. Roxanne could see two cars parked in front of the building, under the tree, taking advantage of the shade.

"Oz and Lisa live on the other side of town," Jack added as more of Tangent came into view.

It seemed impossible that only twenty-four hours had passed since she'd driven out of Tangent. She'd been so filled with what turned out to be ill-founded confidence. She'd been sure she'd have the answer to Dolly's whereabouts before the sun set. She'd even envisioned the call to her grandmother with an update. She'd still have to call sometime today, but with nothing to report.

They passed the courthouse and the motel Roxanne had stayed at.

Gesturing at a low building on the right, Jack added, "Liz was at the party. Remember her? Bright red hair? One of three pregnant ladies sitting under an umbrella? Anyway, she runs the Coffee Corner Diner. Bart is our postmaster and her husband. He was there, too."

"I didn't really get to meet anyone," Roxanne said. "Remember, I ran out on you after you accused me of browbeating Sal."

"That's right," he said, his eyes twinkling again. Through the sheer effort of his conversation, he was turning the mood around inside the car and she was deeply appreciative. "Let me assure you that everyone there was very aware of you, however."

"I bet they were."

"That's my clinic," Jack said as they passed a brick building on the corner. "Nicole used to call it my home away from home."

"Why don't you just live in town?"

He shrugged his broad shoulders and pinned her with another one of his laserlike stares. "The ranch has been in the family for a long time. Except for the horses, I don't

have time to do any of the work, but I want to pass it along
to Ginny someday. Besides, it's peaceful out there. I love
it.''

''I can see why,'' she said, glancing around. There were
exactly eight cars within sight, twelve pedestrians and one
stoplight. ''It must be heaven to escape the hustle-bustle
pressure-cooker pace of this budding metropolis.''

Jack laughed. The sound was so refreshing, so natural,
it blew like a fresh breeze through the luxurious vehicle,
taking with it much of the tension and sadness lodged in
Roxanne's chest.

Within a moment or two, he pulled up in front of a big
metal building. A dusty sign hanging slightly lopsided
above the huge roll-up door read Oz Repair and Towing.

''Their house is around back,'' Jack said, grabbing his
medical bag from the back seat.

At one time in the recent past, someone had tried to
gussy the place up with red geraniums planted in a half-
dozen dirt-filled tires. It might have been charming in its
own garage-type way if the flowers had lived. As it was,
the row of tires each hosted a dead plant and little else.

''I guess they forgot to water,'' Jack said. ''Their attention has been focused elsewhere lately.''

The ''elsewhere'' he referred to became painfully obvious as stereo cries carried through the open screen door.

''Lisa? Oz?'' Jack called as he rapped on the door frame.
''It's me, Jack Wheeler.'' Without waiting for a response,
he opened the door and ushered Roxanne in before him.

The room they entered was small and filled with baby
paraphernalia. An overhead fan provided some relief from
the growing heat of the day but mostly just seemed to scat-
ter the dust. Roxanne stepped over piles of folded baby
clothes, bags of disposable diapers and two identical
bouncy chairs. Her foot came down on a rattle. Not that

she could hear it; the room was also filled with the sound of crying infants.

She found an empty patch of carpet on which to stand while Jack looked into the kitchen. "Lisa?" he called again.

The cries changed pitch—slightly—and a woman's reedy voice said, "Oh, Doc, am I ever glad to see you."

A door behind Roxanne opened. A young man with sandy-colored hair and very light blue eyes, and wearing nothing but tan shorts appeared. Roxanne smiled at him.

He yawned and blinked and scratched his head. "What time is it?" he asked, raising his voice to be heard.

Roxanne didn't have a watch on her sunburned arm. Shrugging, she looked around the room for a clock, but by then the man was making his way over and around things to get to the kitchen. He stopped near Roxanne, introduced himself as Oz, shook her hand and continued on his way. Meanwhile, the cries settled into a dull roar.

Roxanne was amazed that he had been able to sleep with all the noise. She waited for a second, feeling very out of place, then sighed. As everyone seemed to be in the kitchen, she decided she might as well join them.

By the time she crossed the threshold, Jack was holding both babies and their cries had all but petered out. They were butterball children, pink and round, with runny noses and little coughs that erupted now and again but didn't seem dangerous, at least to Roxanne.

Their mother, Lisa, was as fair as the children, but little more than skin and bones. Her jeans rode on jutting hip-bones, her arms looked too frail to handle her babies. Oz looked bewildered by his wife, by his offspring, by life.

Jack, on the other hand, looked quite content. As one baby or the other tugged on his ears, tweaked his nose or pinched his mouth with chubby fingers, he stared gravely at Lisa.

"Are you taking your iron pills?" he said, his voice low and calm. Roxanne felt a shiver run down her spine at the pure *concern* that tone imparted. It must be his doctor voice.

"How about those prenatal vitamins? I want you to continue taking everything I prescribed before the babies were born until you get yourself built back up."

"I try to tell her that, Doc," Oz said.

"Are you eating?" Jack added as he juggled the children.

"I don't have time to shop, let alone eat," Lisa said, her voice high-pitched and wavering.

Jack handed one of the babies to the closest adult, which happened to be Roxanne. She was startled to receive the child whose blue eyes were still filled with tears. The baby wiggled and made a few little grunts. Roxanne immediately began bouncing the child in her arms, determined to keep it from launching back into renewed sobs.

With his now-free hand, Jack opened the refrigerator. Roxanne, who loathed cooking and hardly ever visited a grocery store, was still shocked to see how empty it was. Unless Lisa wanted cold beer, milk, ketchup or what appeared to be a selection of old vegetables, she was out of luck.

Closing the refrigerator, Jack looked at Oz. "Take Lisa on down to the diner and get Liz to make her a patty melt."

"I can't eat a—"

He shushed her with a stern frown. "You need protein and iron. Eat a patty melt. It won't kill you. And a spinach salad. And a milkshake. Then you two go grocery shopping and don't come back here without some decent food. Go on, now."

"But the babies—"

"Roxanne and I will watch the babies. I'll give them a check-up while you're gone and see how their colds are

coming along. Right now I'm more concerned about you.
Have they been fed recently?''

''I just finished.''

''Good. Go.''

Gesturing at Roxanne, Oz said, ''But we can't ask
her—''

''Sure you can,'' Jack said. ''When you get back, she's
going to hit you up for help with her broken-down car and
on a Sunday, too. You'll have plenty of ways to thank her.''

After a few more mild protests, the young couple finally
left. Jack looked at Roxanne rather sheepishly. ''I took a
lot for granted by volunteering you,'' he said. ''I hope you
don't mind.''

''I don't mind,'' she said, admiring the baby's toes. They
were so pudgy and cute, they didn't look real.

Jack cleared off the kitchen table and covered it with a
clean towel he'd grabbed from a shelf, all with a gurgling,
drooling baby held over his arm, then carefully laid the
child on the towel and opened his medical kit.

''This is Amy and that's Sue, or the other way around,
I can't tell them apart,'' Jack said as Roxanne found an
empty chair and sat down. ''They're three months old.
Aren't you, sweetheart?''

Jack was kissing the baby's fingers as he said this, and
the tiny girl gazed back at him adoringly. Jeez, this guy
effortlessly worked his magic on any female, no matter
what her age.

''The big concern is ear infections,'' he added as he
shone a light in first one small ear and then the other. ''I
don't see any signs of one, however.''

''Then why were they crying like that?''

He looked at her and smiled. ''Well, babies cry. Plus,
like lots of twins, these two were born a little early so their
nervous systems are still playing catch-up. They can become overstimulated quite easily. Sometimes, just handing

them to another person or laying them down for a while can soothe them."

"Lisa looked like she was teetering on the edge of a breakdown," Roxanne said.

"Lisa is just barely twenty and Oz is clueless when it comes to balancing work, little kids and looking out for his wife. They're both in over their heads. But I've seen it happen before—they'll adjust."

Roxanne found a tissue and used it to mop her charge's nose. The child really was a cute little thing. She said, "This is the first baby I have ever held."

He lowered a stethoscope. "I can't believe that."

"Honest," she said, laying the baby on her lap, faceup. She held both plump hands in hers and brought them together in a clapping motion. The baby smiled and made a gurgling sound.

"Look, I made her laugh!" Roxanne said, and she glanced up at him, smiling.

He looked at her with the oddest expression on his handsome face. He seemed so large in the cluttered little kitchen, so out of place and yet so at home. She was beginning to think of him as a chameleon, changing colors, as it were, to suit his environment. She had the unreasonable desire to see him…flustered. Ill at ease. Out of his element, if such a place or condition existed.

What a fool he must think she was. Here she was a twenty-seven-year-old woman who had never even held a baby and was giddy now because she'd made one laugh. Her life, which had seemed so important and, well, glamorous a few days before, now seemed artificial. No, that wasn't right. Her life was as real as his was. Her life was just so one-dimensional.

So what?

Not everyone could be a country doctor who swept into a home and ordered people about. He was the man on the white horse, a role he liked, a role that fit him. It would be easy to get swept up in his wake. Maybe that's why his wife left. Maybe she couldn't take being a shadow.

"Let's exchange babies," he said.

Roxanne gave up her little girl and took the other. When the baby coughed, Roxanne held her up against her shoulder and patted her back. She heard soft, comforting noises and realized they were coming from her.

Jack used the phone and talked for a few minutes, his voice courteous but insistent and so soft, she couldn't hear what he was saying. When he hung up, he winked at Roxanne. "Reinforcements will arrive soon," he said mysteriously. After a while, the young couple returned, both of them looking a fraction more composed than when they left.

Oz carried in a few bags of groceries as Jack told Lisa to continue giving the babies the decongestant as needed and not to worry, the babies were going to be fine.

"I called my aunts, Sadie and Veronica," he added. "You know them, right?"

"They used to own the diner," Lisa said.

"That's right. Well, they're getting their driver, George, to bring them over pretty soon. They can hardly wait to get their hands on your babies."

"I couldn't ask—"

"You take a nap while they care for the children—doctor's orders. Oz, Roxanne needs to talk to you."

While Lisa put the groceries away, Roxanne explained to Oz about her car. Jack commented that it appeared she'd cracked the oil pan and Oz nodded. "That won't take but a day or so to replace," he said. "If I have one in stock." He glanced at his wife and the children and sighed. "I'll tow the car into the station this afternoon."

"Tomorrow will be soon enough," Roxanne said. She

wanted her car fixed now but couldn't bring herself to take
Oz from his family.

Looking relieved, he said, "First thing in the morning,
then. You'll be out at Doc's?"

That's where Roxanne wanted to be. How else was she
supposed to wear down Sal's defenses and find out what
she was hiding? But Jack managed to look away the instant
she looked up at him and she realized he didn't want her
there. As she'd already taken advantage of his hospitality
to an alarming degree, she said, "No, I'll get my room back
at the Cactus Gulch."

"Sure, Pete will fix you up fine. They got cable over
there and everything." A note of longing crept into his
voice as he seemed to drift away into thoughts of himself
in a quiet, air-conditioned motel room, with nothing fighting for his attention except cable TV and a soft bed. "I'll
call you in the morning," he added.

As they started to leave, a series of shrill beeps announced Jack's pager. Glancing at it he asked to use the
phone. As he made his call, the babies began to fuss again.

The alarm on Jack's face as he put down the receiver
caused a geyser of concern to spout in Roxanne's chest.
Reason said she didn't know anyone here to worry about.
Reason said this call had nothing to do with her. But reason
didn't have a chance against the instinctual dread that filled
her heart.

Grandma Nell!

"That was Nancy Kaufman," he said in a soft voice so
only Roxanne could hear. "I have to get over to the radio
station right now."

Relief flooded her, weakening her knees. Then she was
beset by apprehension. Though Nancy Kaufman had looked
quite pregnant, it obviously wasn't time to have the baby.
Grabbing his arm, she said, "I'll go with you."

* * *

He drove as fast as he could, glad that it was a Sunday and the streets were fairly empty.

Roxanne sat as tense as a coiled spring beside him. He knew she was darting him quick looks and imagined she was afraid on some level.

He toyed around with the idea of dropping her off at the motel but couldn't bring himself to abandon her like that. Tangent was dead on a Sunday. Even the diner closed down right after lunch. Without transportation, she'd be stuck, alone and worried. He'd get her back to the motel after he checked Nancy.

A few blocks from Lisa and Oz's place, she said, "Will Nancy be okay?"

"She'll be fine," he said, crossing his mental fingers that it was so. The truth was that Nancy and Paul had been trying to have children for years. Even her age, forty in a year or so, put her pregnancy in the high-risk category.

He and Nancy had gone to school together. They'd even dated one summer when they were both teetering on sixteen. He took what happened to her very personally. If it meant moving heaven and earth to save the baby and safeguard Nancy, he'd do it.

"Is it the baby?"

"Yes."

"Is it serious?"

He reached out and covered Roxanne's hand with his own. "Probably not. She's having contractions. Please, try not to worry. We'll be there in a few minutes."

Roxanne rubbed her temple with her free hand. He noticed that she made no move to withdraw her hand from his casual grip. He assumed his touch relaxed her. As focused as he was on getting to Nancy and assessing the situation, he still felt anything but relaxed when touching Roxanne.

She made every nerve ending in his body prickle.

This was absolutely outrageous and he knew it. With every fiber of his being he wanted to cast her out of the car. With every fiber of his being he wanted to explore the new sensations she aroused.

New? For a man sliding toward forty himself, a man with a failed marriage in his past?

Yeah, new.

Pretty soon it was time to make the turn into the long dirt driveway leading to the radio station, and Roxanne slipped her hand from his. He grabbed the steering wheel.

They found Nancy lying on a couch in one of three rooms that comprised the small station. A teenage boy he recognized hovered nearby, wringing his hands. The relief he felt upon seeing Jack was palatable.

"Doc," the boy said, rushing forward.

Jack thumped him on the shoulder. "It's okay, Tony."

Nancy looked more irritated than scared. "Honestly, Jack, it's just a few Braxton-Hicks contractions."

"Has your water broken?"

"No. See? It's nothing."

"If it's nothing, then why did you call?"

"Because I made her," Tony said. "My mom had a baby at home. Dad had to deliver it. I don't know how to deliver a baby!"

Out of the corner of his eye, he saw Roxanne hide a smile behind her hand.

Jack said, "Don't worry, you're off the hook. Okay, Nancy, how bad are the contractions?"

"Not too bad. I'll come into your office first thing in the morning. I promise."

As he fished a stethoscope out of his bag he was vaguely aware of Roxanne talking to the boy, leading him off to the far side of the room, her voice brisk and efficient and commanding.

Jack put the stethoscope down. "I hear a fetal heart-beat," he assured Nancy.

"See? Everything is fine." Her eyes got wide for a moment, she clutched her stomach and began panting. When the contraction was over, Jack helped her into a sitting position.

"I'm sorry," he told her, "but we need to get you to the hospital. We'll hook you up to a fetal monitor and see how the baby is responding to all this. That way, if this is the beginning of labor, you'll be where you should be."

"I don't think I can drive."

"Of course you can't drive. Where's Paul?"

"Off fishing with the Boise brothers. I don't even know for sure where they are."

"Then I'll take you. We're not going to take any chances. I'm driving you into the hospital."

"But the clinic—"

"Isn't equipped to handle an emergency," he said softly. "Don't stop trusting me now, okay?"

She nodded, her eyes glistening.

He stood up. Roxanne was close by and it was obvious she'd heard what was going on. "I'll stay here," she said. "Tony and I will keep the station running while you're gone, Nancy. Don't worry about a thing."

Jack said, "Where's Tony?"

"I told him to go boil water on the hot plate."

Jack smiled. "You watch too much television," he said.

"Hey, it's my job to watch too much television." She leaned down and tenderly grasped Nancy's shoulder. "I know we really haven't met, Nancy. I'm Roxanne and I just want you to know that I interned at a small radio station up in Washington during college. Lots of your equipment seems to be the same vintage as what I'm used to. I know the tape that's running right now will be off in a few minutes. Tony and I will do fine."

"Tony's new," Nancy said, her voice trembling. It was as though the potential seriousness of her situation was finally sinking in. "There's nobody for you to call—I made everyone take their vacations before my due date. Teresa could take over, but she's in Alaska with her husband for another week or so. Hank doesn't like to figure out the programming, but he'll be back tomorrow for the afternoon/evening shift. I always start things out in the morning except on Sundays when I do a shortened day. Reverend Thomas does forty-five minutes today starting at twelve-fifteen. There's a log on the computer you can follow. I'm hooked up to the United Press Wire for the news—"

"Don't worry," Roxanne repeated. "I'll stay until reinforcements arrive or until sign-off. Everything will be fine."

Jack leaned down and helped Nancy stand. She grimaced and he knew she was fighting another mild contraction. The tears began rolling down her cheeks and he felt that old well of frustration mount in his gut.

Roxanne opened doors, her manner confident and assured. When Nancy was safely tucked into the car and the door closed, he turned to Roxanne. "Thank you—"

"It's okay."

"I hate to leave you like this—"

"Don't be silly."

"We'll be at the hospital in Helpern. If her husband shows up—"

"I'll send him winging on his way."

For a fraction of a second longer, he stared at her. There was so much he wanted to say, so much that had been gathering in his subconscious all morning. In a flash he saw her holding Ginny's hand, bouncing the fretful baby, comforting Nancy. There was so much he wanted to tell her but he didn't have the time or the words. He felt as though he was choking and he knew he needed a clear mind for what lay ahead. "Roxanne—" he began.

She reached up quickly and kissed his mouth. Her lips were warm and intoxicating. He was stunned as much by the spontaneity of her gesture as by the mere fact that she'd been the one to initiate a kiss, brief and rushed as it was.

"It's okay," she whispered.

Jack got into the car. He could see Roxanne's slight figure in the rearview mirror as he drove away. As if she knew he was watching her, she raised one hand for a second before turning around and reentering the station.

Chapter Six

At the top of the hour, Roxanne read the news as per instructions from the log on the computer screen. After that, she played three prerecorded national commercials, read two local ones live, then created a segue into a segment entitled, "A Word with Reverend Thomas."

"For those of you listening this afternoon and wondering where Nancy Kaufman is," Roxanne said, speaking into the microphone, "worry not. She'll be back soon. My name is Roxanne Salyer, a stranger to your lovely town, and I'm pleased to introduce a man I hear needs no introduction as he shares his wisdom with you every Sunday. Reverend Thomas, it's all yours."

Reverend Jeremy Thomas was a tall, gangly redhead with a natural skin tone pinker than Roxanne's sunburn. Roxanne left as he began talking in a very mellow, smooth voice that added twenty years to his age. Tony was sitting on a chair, staring at her, awaiting direction.

"What do you normally do?" she asked him.

He was almost as tall as the reverend, but his eyes were

black, his skin was a golden tanned color and his dark hair was shaved close to the scalp.

"Mrs. Kaufman just hired me to do an after-school music thing, you know, for kids and all. I was just in here today watching her, kind of like learning the ropes, you know?"

"I know. I did the same thing when I was younger. Well, I guess you can watch the reverend, and after he's through, you can help me play some nice mellow music to fill the hour until we put on the old soap opera. After that I see that Nancy does forty minutes of household hints, more music, slide on in to home plate with a big sign-off. Tomorrow, show up at three o'clock as planned. I see on the log that Hank Kimball is taking over the early-afternoon shift while Teresa is on vacation. Then he stays around for his own show and closes things up."

"I stay an hour after my shift to sweep the floor and dust."

"Okay. Well, let's look at the tape files. I can't take over Nancy's household hint show."

"She just tells people how to get their clothes whiter and stuff like that."

Roxanne, smiling, said, "I don't know how to get clothes whiter, do you, Tony?"

He grinned. "All I know about is parakeets."

"Parakeets?"

"I raise them. I've got lots of babies right now—you should see them."

Roxanne laughed. "Of course you have baby parakeets. This whole town is full of babies! You don't happen to have ever heard of a woman called Dolly Aames, have you?"

He looked perplexed. "Nope."

"It was a long shot. Okay, show me where Nancy keeps the tapes."

Paul Kaufman, Nancy's husband, showed up at the station midway through the soap opera. By the way Paul burst through the door, Roxanne assumed he'd been listening to the radio. Finding Roxanne holding down the fort did nothing to wipe the anxious expression off his face.

"I couldn't find a phone. It was quicker just to come—where's Nancy?"

"Jack took her to the hospital in Helpern. He said you should drive down there."

"Is she...is the baby..."

"They were both fine when they left here, Mr. Kaufman."

He turned abruptly and was gone.

Eventually Tony went home to tend to his parakeets, and after that, it was time to play the "Star Spangled Banner." Roxanne closed down shop with a feeling of accomplishment. She'd skirted through the afternoon without a single major mishap.

And without even once thinking about Jack Wheeler except in the detached manner she'd relayed information to Paul Kaufman. She'd been able to put him clean out of her mind—not an easy accomplishment. But now, with the task at hand taken care of, he came marching back in, demanding attention. Just like him.

Giving in to temptation, she thought about the way he'd looked at her outside Nancy's car and the way his lips had responded when she kissed him. She thought of the vulnerable look in his eyes as he tried to tell her something, and the thankful look when she let him off the hook.

She suspected he was beginning to care for her in the same way she was beginning to care for him. Logic told her this was a mistake on both their parts—they lived hundreds and hundreds of miles apart with separate careers. Besides all that, Jack was a man with baggage.

He had a very full life, consisting of family, friends and townsfolk, all of whom seemed to also be his patients. He had a young daughter who needed him. But most of all, he had the memory of his fickle ex-wife, and Roxanne had the feeling he used Nicole as a measuring stick for all the other no-good women he met.

So, maybe he did look as though he wanted to grab her and kiss her, and maybe she wished with all her heart that he would—the bottom line didn't change because of hormones or lust. The bottom line was that caring too much for each other was a mistake.

Plain and simple, except that there was nothing plain and simple about it.

It wasn't until she'd printed out the log of the day's events and stacked it in with all the others, that she realized she was stuck. Her money and suitcase were in Jack's car, she was a mile or so outside of Tangent. Without money, she couldn't hire a cab and really, it was hard to imagine Tangent even had taxi service. The only people she knew were Oz and Lisa, and there was no way on earth she was going to call them and ask for help.

The phone rang just as she considered the possibility of walking into town—something she really didn't want to do. It was Jack.

"I'm on the car phone," he said, "just a few minutes out of town. I was hoping you were still there. I'll give you a ride."

"Great," she said as though she had a hundred other options.

After unplugging the coffee machine and rinsing out the pot, she found a key hanging on a hook by the door and locked the station, then began walking down the driveway toward the main highway. It felt good to stretch her legs. Apparently she wasn't the first to make this trek on foot as she found a bright copper penny on the road and picked it up.

Found pennies always made her think of Grandma Nell.

As soon as Roxanne got to the motel, she had to call her grandmother and report…nothing.

Jack's car came into view within minutes and she hooked out a thumb. He slowed down and she got into the air-conditioned, plush leather interior with a sigh.

"How's Nancy?"

"Better," he said. "We've got her on medication. She's going to be bedridden for the rest of her pregnancy. Maybe in the hospital."

"Did her husband ever get there?"

"That's what took me so long. I didn't want to leave until Paul showed up. He said he was listening to the radio when he heard you say Nancy was away. He couldn't imagine where she'd gone until you told him."

"But the baby is okay?"

"For now. A prenatal expert is going to see her tomorrow. All we want to do is keep the baby right where it is for as long as possible."

By now they were driving on the main highway. It took Roxanne a few seconds to figure out they were heading away from town. When she pointed this out, Jack cast her a quick glance.

"I'm taking you to my house. The diner is closed. If you stay at the motel, your dinner will have to come from the Handy-Mart. I assume you didn't have lunch and I wouldn't condemn anyone to their fried chicken."

Roxanne, who was delighted to be getting another chance to quiz Sal, felt irritation, as well. "Maybe I like fried chicken," she said. "Maybe I already have a reservation at the Cactus Gulch Motel. Maybe you should ask people what they want before just telling them. I'm not one of your patients."

"So you want me to take you into town?"

Pride made her snap, "Yes."

He slowed the car down and pulled to the side of the

The Silhouette Reader Service™ — Here's how it works:

ccepting your 2 free books and gift places you under no obligation to buy anything. You may keep the books and gift nd return the shipping statement marked "cancel." If you do not cancel, about a month later we'll send you 6 additional ovels and bill you just $2.90 each in the U.S., or $3.25 each in Canada, plus 25¢ shipping & handling per book and pplicable taxes if any.* That's the complete price and — compared to cover prices of $3.50 each in the U.S. and $3.99 ach in Canada — it's quite a bargain! You may cancel at any time, but if you choose to continue, every month we'll send ou 6 more books, which you may either purchase at the discount price or return to us and cancel your subscription.

Terms and prices subject to change without notice. Sales tax applicable in N.Y. Canadian residents will be charged pplicable provincial taxes and GST.

Play The *Lucky Hearts* Game

and get...

FREE BOOKS & a FREE GIFT... YOURS to KEEP!

Yes! I have scratched off the silver card. Please send me my **2 FREE BOOKS** and **FREE MYSTERY GIFT**. I understand that I am under no obligation to purchase any books as explained on the back of this card.

Scratch Here!
then look below to see what your cards get you...

DETACH AND MAIL CARD TODAY! (S-R-OS-05/01)

© 1998 HARLEQUIN ENTERPRISES LTD. ® and TM are trademarks owned by Harlequin Books S.A. used under license.

315 SDL DC4C   **215 SDL DC36**

NAME   (PLEASE PRINT CLEARLY)

ADDRESS

APT.#   CITY

STATE/PROV.   ZIP/POSTAL CODE

Twenty-one gets you **2 FREE BOOKS** and a **FREE MYSTERY GIFT!**

Twenty gets you **2 FREE BOOKS!**

Nineteen gets you **1 FREE BOOK!**

TRY AGAIN!

Offer limited to one per household and not valid to current Silhouette Romance® subscribers. All orders subject to approval.

Visit us online at

www.eHarlequin.com

road. Turning in his seat, he fixed her with a stare that lit fires behind her eyeballs. Then he said, "Let's start over. Roxanne, I have an idea. Since the diner is closed and the cooking grease at the Handy-Mart hasn't been changed since 1982, would you do me the honor of coming to my house for dinner?"

Stifling a smile, she said, "All right. Since you ask so nicely."

With that, they were off again.

All Roxanne could think of was a bath with some of that soothing gel added to the water, clean clothes and shoes that fit. Then a cold drink and something to eat. And maybe a glimpse of Ginny and a long talk with Sal. And Jack. She wanted to know what he'd been trying to say when he'd left her that day. She wanted to know what he thought about her impulsive kiss. She wanted him to kiss her back.

He said, "I feel a sense of peace as soon as I leave town behind."

This time she didn't make fun of his idea of what constituted a town. The man was well educated—obviously he'd been in big cities before. Instead she said, "I'm surprised you don't ride one of the horses to work, Jack."

He chuckled. "I would if I could. Horseback is a wonderful way to get around."

"You should have been a cowboy."

"I know. I take it you don't ride."

She cast him a quick glance. "Hard to ride a horse when you've never seen one up close and personal. Until yesterday, that was me. But I like your horses. I wouldn't mind taking one for a spin."

He laughed again. "A horse isn't a sports car, Roxanne."

"Think about it," she teased. "Convertible top, seats two in a pinch, corners well—"

"You're a nut," he told her with a devastating smile, as

though he enjoyed nuts. They were grinning at each other when they pulled into his ranch. The grins faded quickly as chaos met their eyes. They both put down their windows as the car rolled to a stop.

A blue truck sat in the middle of the yard. The passenger door was open, Carl was outside the door and Grace was inside. Sal was holding what appeared to be a blanket and Ginny was running around the group, yelling. All heads swiveled toward the car pulling alongside them.

"What the—" Jack began, but Carl rushed ahead, his speech a torrent of words.

"Grace is bleeding, Doc. Not a lot. I shouldn't have taken her out to Deadman's Canyon. It's my fault."

"Carl, honey, shut up," Grace said.

Roxanne smiled to herself. She was beginning to admire the women in this town.

"It's just a little spotting, that's all," she added. "I keep telling you all I'm fine."

"What about the baby, Doc?" Carl said, worry dripping from his words.

"I'll check her over, Carl. Calm down."

"She shouldn't get a chill," Sal said, flinging the blanket over Grace's shoulders.

It had to be nearly ninety degrees outside, Roxanne thought, but kept quiet.

Ginny ran up to the car and said, "Daddy, did you bring me something?"

"Not now, sweetpea," he said as he got out of the car. Roxanne followed suit. "Carl, why don't you carry Grace to your room?"

"I've put on a little weight," Grace announced as Carl advanced. "Just let me walk."

"No," Carl said, still advancing.

"It's okay, Carl. She can walk if she wants to," Jack

said. Looking down at Roxanne, he added in a whisper, "Stubborn woman."

"Independent woman," Roxanne said sweetly.

Since her help wasn't needed, Roxanne took her suitcases into the house and down the hall. Opening doors, she finally found a room that was obviously kept just for guests. She settled for a quick shower—bliss—and a change of clothes. Dressed in her own shorts and sleeveless halter top, she felt comfortable for the first time in two days. A pair of worn sneakers made her feel as if she were walking on sponge cake.

The room also boasted a telephone, and using her calling card, Roxanne phoned home.

"Gran? How are you feeling?"

"Pretty good," Grandma Nell said, her voice unusually subdued.

"Is Linda taking good care of you?"

"She hovers and her silly parrot jabbers day and night. Where are you, honey?"

"I'm in Tangent."

There was a hush on the other end before a whispered, "Did you find Dolly?"

"Not yet, Gran."

"Do you have a lead? Did you show someone my letter and her picture? I know she's down there somewhere. I can feel it in my bones."

Roxanne had intended to start letting her grandmother down easy by hinting that this was not only a very cold trail but a dead end. However, when faced with the hope she could hear in Gran's voice, she just couldn't do it. "I do have a lead," she said, exaggerating her hunch that Sal knew something she wasn't telling. "I'll call you in a day or so, maybe with more news. Gran, you said her parents died when she was seventeen. Wasn't there anyone else around?"

"No one I ever knew of."

"Where was she from originally?"

"I just can't remember. Maybe Oregon, maybe California, but I can't recall any names. Now, you hug Dolly for me when you find her. And tell her I want to see her. I want to get all us old gals together for one last song. Tell her that."

"Gran, don't get your hopes up too high. It's been a long time. Dolly is bound to have changed—"

"Nonsense! She'll be the same sweet girl, you'll see," she said, excusing herself for a second. Roxanne heard the muffled sound of a cough.

"Are you eating, Gran?"

"I don't have much of an appetite lately—you know that. It's just because I'm…well, preoccupied. Besides, Linda is a lousy cook. She boils canned beans for forty-five minutes until they're like mush. I tell her I still have my teeth, but she does it anyway."

Roxanne's smile was short-lived.

"Truth is," Gran added in a rare moment of vulnerability, "I'm a little scared."

"I know you are, but everything is going to be fine. You'll get that X ray on Wednesday and it won't show a darn thing. You'll see."

Back to her old practical self, Gran said, "This call must be costing you a fortune. Hang up now."

"I love you," Roxanne said as she replaced the receiver. The tears started immediately, running like raindrops down her cheeks.

Grandma Nell had never before, not once during the long months of her illness, not during surgery, chemotherapy or radiation admitted to being afraid. Was it an omen? And that cough—was it worse?

Roxanne found Ginny sitting outside the guest room door

when she finally let herself out. The little girl's lower lip was trembling and her eyes were watery.

"What's the matter?" Roxanne asked, kneeling down.

"Daddy didn't bring me anything."

Roxanne sighed. "Well, honey, he's had a very busy day."

"He said he would bring me a surprise."

Roxanne had a sudden thought. "I brought you something instead. Is that okay?"

The pouty lip disappeared. "You did? What?"

Roxanne walked back into the guest room. Opening the closet, she found the black dress she'd put on a hanger, and reached into one of the side-slit pockets. She smiled as her fingers touched the penny she'd found earlier.

"A penny?" Ginny said. Her voice made it clear she wasn't impressed.

"Not just any penny…a special penny," Roxanne said. She sat down on the bed and the child crawled up next to her, leaning against Roxanne in a manner so innocent and so beguiling that it made Roxanne's heart swell.

"My grandma Nell calls these 'Found Pennies,'" Roxanne said with a catch in her throat. "When you find a penny like this, you put it in a very secret place. That makes it a magical-wish penny. If you save every penny you find, then someday, when you have a whole bunch of them, you get to make a really special wish and it will come true."

As a child, the story had always made perfect sense to Roxanne. In fact, she still had a big jar of "Found Pennies" at home. But saying it aloud for the first time in her life, she saw it really raised more questions than it answered.

And yet, in the back of her mind, a thought emerged. Should she rush home and find her pennies and make that one special wish? Did she have to be holding the pennies? Could she do it long-distance? Did the magical pennies have to be in the same room, in the same state, on the same planet?

I wish Gran peace and health, she whispered inside her heart.

"You're crying," Ginny said.

Roxanne hadn't realized she'd closed her eyes. She wiped away the telltale tears with shaky fingers, at a loss as to what to say to explain them to the child staring at her with alarm in her blue eyes.

"You better keep the penny," Ginny said, handing it back.

That simple statement, uttered with complete faith that it would make everything better, actually elicited more tears. Folding Ginny's hand over the coin, Roxanne said, "No, sweetheart, I want you to have it."

"I have a secret place," Ginny whispered.

"Do you?"

The child scooted off the bed. She turned at the door, issuing, with her eyes, an invitation for Roxanne to follow. Ginny went down the hall into her room and right over to a pink box. When she opened it, the tinkling tune of "I Could Have Danced All Night" played as a ballerina twirled around and around and around.

"There you two are," Jack said.

Roxanne turned. Her first thought was how gloriously the man filled a domestic doorway. From the bottom of his shoes, up his long legs, almost to the top of his sunbleached brown hair. From broad shoulders to tapered hips, doorways were meant to be dominated by men like Jack Wheeler.

Her second thought was of her own face, and she hastily raised her fingers to wipe away the last of the tears that had snaked down her cheeks.

He smiled at her, then dropped his gaze to Ginny. "Listen, sweetpea, I'm sorry I forgot to bring you something like I said I would—"

"It's okay," Ginny said, depositing her penny and closing her box. The music clicked off.

"It is?"

Ginny nodded, then glancing up at Roxanne, added, "Roxanne brought me something instead."

"What did she bring you?" Jack said, advancing into the room, his gaze piercing Roxanne's equilibrium. He looked from her to Ginny, the gleam of curiosity in his eyes. He was still dressed in slacks and a white shirt, and even after the day he'd put in, Roxanne thought he looked vibrant and one hundred and fifty percent alive.

"It's a secret," she said.

"Even from your dad?"

"It's not a secret if I tell everyone."

He bent down and hefted her into his arms. "Since when am I everyone? Come on, don't make me tickle you."

Ginny laughed and wriggled free. "I'm hungry."

The thought of a hungry child and no cook apparently chased Jack's curiosity away. "Uh—well, Grace is in bed, and Sal is taking charge of babying her, so I guess it's up to us to fix something." He looked at Roxanne and added, "Can you cook?"

"Sure," she said. She didn't add that cooking to her meant opening a can or throwing something frozen into the microwave. "Let's see what you've got."

Jack washed the last of the dinner dishes. The meal had raised more than a few eyebrows in the house, among them, Sal's, Grace's and Carl's. But Ginny had loved the idea of scrambled eggs, leftover fruit balls and toaster pastry for dinner, and truth of the matter was that it filled the empty spot in his stomach just fine. Besides, Roxanne had been a good sport to cook—it was obvious that she didn't know her way around a kitchen, and he found it kind of endearing that she went ahead and tried without complaining.

Somewhere in the back of his mind, a warning bell went off.

Roxanne had volunteered to put Ginny to bed. Sal was caring for Grace while Carl took care of chores out of doors. He realized he was in something of a domestic crunch.

After the dishes, he called the hospital and reassured himself that Nancy Kaufman was resting comfortably and that Paul was still there with her. Then he checked on Grace, ordered Sal to bed and went searching for his daughter.

He found her asleep in her bed, her arm around her birthday music box. The lid was open, but the ballerina had long since wound down and he could see a bright penny in the bottom where jewelry was meant to go. Of course, like most three-year-old girls, Ginny didn't have much jewelry. He wondered where she'd gotten the penny.

He kissed her forehead, then carefully extracted the box, depositing it on her dresser before leaving the pink-and-white room. The colors had been her choice—it continually amazed him that a child who was such a tomboy outside was so feminine inside. Ginny was all girl, in the modern sense of the word. Rough and tumble, obstinate and loving, fond of dolls and snakes; she was clever, goofy and sweet.

As he moved down the hall, his brain made the transition from thinking about his daughter to contemplating Roxanne. He wanted to find her. He *needed* to find her.

There was the matter of that impetuous kiss to be dealt with.

There was the matter of the way she'd looked standing next to Ginny. And the way she'd looked at him.

He peeked in the guest room she'd told him she'd commandeered, but she wasn't there. He thought about the barn and the animals she seemed to like so much, but something made him step out into the courtyard.

The night air was heavy with the smells of the desert and the flowers that overflowed the broad terra-cotta planters he'd bought in Mexico a decade before. A figure was seated by the fountain. He didn't need to see the gold dust reflected in her pale hair to know at whom he was looking. Crazy as it would sound to anyone with an ounce of brains, he could *feel* Roxanne's presence.

"May I join you?" he called, closing the door behind him.

She stood abruptly, as though yanked from her thoughts. "Jack."

"Mind if I turn on a light?" he added.

"Go ahead," she said.

He flipped on a switch and the underwater light in the fountain came to life. The thing had been created by one of Nicole's designer friends, and he had to hand it to the woman. The effect of the moonlit sky overhead and the soft light sparkling through the water below was beautiful. The effect of both these light sources glancing off the face and figure of the young woman before him was nothing less than magical.

As he approached, she said, "Did you check on Grace again?"

"Yes, she's fine, but Carl may need resuscitation."

"He's just a concerned husband and soon-to-be father. I think it's sweet."

"Wait a second, what happened to all this independent woman stuff?"

"They're married."

"Oh, I see. Once there's a marriage license, then a man gets to boss a woman around?"

"No. Once there's a marriage license, they both get to boss each other around. Isn't that the way it works?"

"I don't have the slightest idea."

"But you were married," she said softly as she perched
on the brick edge of the fountain. She looked from him to
the water, and he had the sense she was avoiding his gaze.
The halter top she wore had a deep and inviting V-shaped
neckline. The lights and shadows highlighted her exquisite
bone structure and the rounded curves of her breasts. Jack
was finding it hard to swallow.

"And now I'm divorced," he said at last. "I'm not a
good one to give advice about marriage. Besides, didn't
you just tell me today that you don't want to get married?"

She glanced back up at him. "I don't believe I said it
quite that way."

"Maybe you were just telling me to mind my own business."

"And not assume things," she said softly.

Jack wondered what Roxanne Salyer would do if he put
his arms around her and kissed her. It was on the tip of his
tongue to ask, but she spoke first.

"Is every pregnancy this complicated?"

He sat down beside her. "You mean Nancy? Absolutely
not. Most are boring as all get out."

"But Grace—"

"We're being cautious because of the miscarriage last
year. I shouldn't have let her work so hard for Ginny's
party. A week or two off her feet and she'll be good as
new."

"But how are you going to get along here for a week or
two without Grace? Who will care for Ginny?"

"I don't know," he said with a sigh. "Sal, I guess. Except Ginny's too much for Sal to handle on a constant basis
so I'll get Sal to care for Grace and find someone in town
who can come out here and care for Ginny and run a mop
around the floors. And cook. Someone is going to have to
cook."

"Me," Roxanne said with a quick upsweep of lashes.

"You, cook?"

"I can cook. I mean, I can learn. Besides, there's a lot more you need done around here than cooking."

His mind raced. What logical, polite excuse could he come up with on the spur of the moment that would dissuade her? He didn't want her around Sal. That was why his pulse had suddenly started pounding, right?

It had nothing to do with the thought of Roxanne living under the same roof. It had nothing to do with the memory of her creamy thigh and that wisp of black lace he'd glimpsed.

He mumbled, "You have a job in Seattle."

"I have two weeks off," she said with another swift glance. "And you have been nothing but kind to me. I owe you."

"No, Roxanne, it doesn't work like that. You don't owe me anything."

"Don't be absurd. Of course I do."

"Anyway," he added, "you're searching for Dolly Aames."

"I have no leads except for your former nanny, Jack, and you know it. I don't know how long you were listening this morning, but Sal knows something. I'm determined to find out what it is."

"You are formidable," he said with a sigh. "Tenacious. Relentless."

"Flattery will get you everywhere."

"I don't think I meant it as flattery."

She took a deep breath and he steeled himself for her next argument. "Tell me what I have to say or do to make it so you'll let me stay here and watch after Ginny, help with Nancy's radio station until Teresa gets back from Alaska and discreetly question Sal?"

He laughed. "Honestly, Roxanne. And you talk about me making decisions for people!"

"I'm serious," she replied.

"I know you are."

"Ginny doesn't know me, that's true, but I don't think she's afraid of me."

Afraid of her? Was she joking? He looked closely at her lovely face and found only earnest speculation. He said, "I agree, Ginny isn't afraid of you."

"And I liked being at the radio station today. I can help Nancy, I know I can. I don't think she'd mind."

"No," he said, chuckling to himself at the understatement, "she wouldn't mind. In fact, it would take a lot of the stress off her, which is what we want."

"See? And three whole hours on the air—it boggles my imagination. Think of what I can do! I'll take Ginny into the studio with me. It'll work, you'll see."

Alarmed by her determination, to say nothing of her plan, he said, "That's all well and good except for Sal."

"Let me talk to her. Don't always rush in. I promise I won't hurt her."

He thought for a moment. Roxanne was giving far more than she was asking. If it was anyone else but Sal, he'd let them take their chances with this dynamo of a television producer. But it wasn't—it was Sal. And though he understood how protective Roxanne felt toward her grandmother, she had to understand he felt the same way about Sal.

"Sal has suffered enough tragedy in her life," he said.

"What do you mean?"

He shook his head. He shouldn't have said even that much. He added, "How about a compromise?"

"Such as?"

"Such as you get to stay here and do all sorts of work for room and board—what a vacation!—and in return *I'll* talk to Sal."

"*You'll* talk to Sal."

"Yes. I promise."

Narrowing her eyes, she said, "You promise."

"Solemn oath."

After more staring, she finally said, "I'll give you a week."

"Two weeks."

"At the end of two weeks I have to go home. If Sal comes up with a lead, I won't have time to follow it. How about nine days? I'll go along with this on the condition that if, within nine days you haven't managed to get Sal to tell you why she backpedals when it comes to answering my questions, then I get to talk to her without you and your white horse."

"Sprite? What's Sprite got to do with it?"

"Not Sprite, Jack. The white horse you figuratively ride around on all the time."

After a moment, he said, "Oh, okay."

They were both silent. He didn't know what she was thinking—he was wondering who had just gotten the better deal. He had a feeling she'd bested him, though he couldn't quite see how.

"What a day," he said at last.

"And this was just a Sunday. I can't imagine what your workdays are like."

"Not as exciting as all this," he said, looping his arms around one bent knee. She had returned her gaze to the fountain. "I bet your workdays are busy, too," he added.

She shrugged.

"Tell me what you do."

"I'm the producer for the *Midday Show*."

"What's the *Midday Show* and what exactly does a producer do?"

"It's ninety minutes of news and local information and stories. I orchestrate things. I select topics for shows, run them by Leon—he's my boss—arrange for guests and interview them, write the scripts and segues...stuff like that.''

"That must give you quite a forum."

"Leon shoots down half of what I suggest. In fact, it's occurred to me lately that the only way I'm going to get what I want out of this job is to take over Leon's position."

"Yikes. Watch out, Leon!"

She laughed. For pure beauty, the sound rivaled the falling water.

"You're ambitious," he said.

"Yes. Aren't you?"

He laughed this time. "Look around you," he said quietly, hopefully without ego because he truly was humbled by his life. "I have everything a man could want. I have a child I adore, a career I find ultimately fulfilling, friends, family, a home that's been in my family for generations." He looked up at the stars bathed in moonlight and added, "And just take a look at the size of that sky!"

"That's yours, too?"

"Every square inch of it," he said. "As you can see, I have it all."

"To say nothing of enough baby animals to populate one of your better petting zoos."

"Exactly."

"I guess it's all your birthright, huh?"

"No," he said. "I was actually born on the coast in Northern California, in a little town named Arcata. My mother was staying with a relative when I was born."

"That must have been exciting for your parents, having a baby so far from home."

"Dad was down here. He saw me for the first time when he came up to get my mother. There are pictures of the three of us standing in front of an airplane."

"You've been wanted and loved your whole life," Roxanne said wistfully.

"Almost. Don't forget the years I spent with Nicole. She did her best to take me down a notch or two."

"Did she succeed?"

"More or less. A man doesn't have his wife run out on him without suffering a little humiliation. It's a rather public way to announce the romance is over."

"And since she left?"

"Romance?" He laughed softly. "I think that part of my life is on hold."

"You think it is or you know it is?"

"Are you always this persistent, Roxanne?"

"Almost always."

"Turnaround is fair play. What happened with the boyfriend?"

For a few moments, he didn't think she was going to answer him. Finally she mumbled, "He broke up with me."

"What is he, nuts?"

She laughed softly. "Thanks. But no, he's not nuts. In some ways, he's kind of like you. He wants what you have—a home, a family. In other words, he wants a wife. He didn't think I was wife material."

"He sounds demented."

"He's a very good-looking news anchor on the evening news. He's thirty-two years old, never been married. Usually you hear about women hearing their biological clock ticking, but I think Kevin heard his. He wants a baby. He met my mother once, he knows how ambivalent I am about her. His parting shot to me was that I'm career driven. He said I'm just like my mother."

"Do you believe that?"

"I don't know. Maybe."

"Do you want the things he wants?"

"A baby? A spouse? I don't know. Not if I'm like my mother. You just pointed out that I'm ambitious. Maybe it's in my genes. Maybe I don't really have a choice. Well, I'm here to tell you it's lonely growing up the way I did. I wouldn't want to wish it on anyone else."

He took a chance. He reached for her hand and held it firmly, running his thumb across her knuckles. The warmth of her hand in his spread up his arm and zapped his heart like a stun gun. With his other hand, he cupped her chin and turned her face to his.

"You kissed me today," he said.

She attempted to turn her face away. When he held firm, she tried to withdraw her hand. It was all done with little pulls and twists, and once she met gentle resistance, she immediately ceased. He wasn't going to let her off the hook.

"You—you looked as though you needed a kiss," she said.

"Funny, that's exactly how you look now."

"No—"

"Yes," he whispered, lowering his face to hers.

Her lips were soft, so soft. How could any two lips be that tender? He pressed into them harder, and he felt her melt against him, her breasts against his arm and chest, her thigh against his thigh. Her surrender surprised and enflamed him. All parts of his body went on alert, reacting like a horde of volunteer firemen to a raucous alarm.

"Roxanne," he muttered against the peachy texture of her cheek. And then he kissed her again, pulling her slender but surprisingly yielding body as close as possible. He buried one hand in her lush hair, kissed her exposed throat, ran his fingers lightly across her halter top. Her nipples were hard beneath the fabric. Her rising excitement met his, he could feel it in her kiss, taste it on her tongue. The alarms were going off so loud now that he couldn't think.

Why should he think? Where had thinking ever gotten him? But he was a thinking man, and shutting down his head to give his body free license wasn't his style. It was just a kiss...well, a series of kisses. Just one more...or a dozen...

Did she sense his hesitation? She cupped his face and moved mere inches away. Her perception made her all the more desirable and he ordered his brain to take a hike. He wanted her close again. Closer.

But it was too late. She stared at him with a speculative look in her deep eyes. "This isn't a good idea," she mumbled. Putting a finger against his lips, she added, "I enjoyed kissing you. But it's not enough."

"Why isn't it?" he asked, speaking against her finger.

"Because of who you are and who I am." Moving her hand, she leaned forward and kissed him again. Her lips seemed to touch and linger—he would have found it extremely alluring if it wasn't so obviously a last kiss, a goodnight kiss.

She rose quickly and left silently. He watched her retreating form with as much regret as he'd ever watched anything in his life.

Jumping to his feet and rubbing his mouth with the back of his hand, he asked himself how this could possibly be so. He'd known this woman thirty-six hours. He'd kissed her a couple of times and held a couple of outrageous conversations with her. She'd bullied Sal and wormed her way into his daughter's life. Now she was fixing to move into his guest bedroom and take over the local airwaves. Roxanne Salyer was a one-woman locust invasion!

And he couldn't get the taste, the feel, the sight of her out of his mind. He had never felt so much confusion, desire and anxiety at one time, not even after Nicole ran off.

After Nicole ran off... The way Roxanne would when her curiosity was satisfied?

He swore softly. With a sinking heart, he decided something. If he wasn't enough for her, then she damn well wasn't enough for him. Hadn't he traveled this road before? "Not again," he whispered. "Never again."

Chapter Seven

Roxanne felt nervous walking into Tangent's only real grocery store, which happened to be kitty-corner to Jack's clinic. He probably came into the store on a daily basis since it was so handy. His feet had no doubt helped wear down the beige linoleum.

She had avoided him that morning just as she wished to avoid him now. All she had to do was push Ginny around in the cart and find something she was capable of fixing for dinner. She wasn't sure how she would stay out of Jack's way once they were both back at the house, but at least they would have privacy for whatever did happen.

Like him asking her to leave?

If she had the night before to do over again, boy, would she do things differently. For starters, she should have nipped their conversation in the bud as soon as he agreed to let her stay for a few days. That's all she wanted—the chance to find Dolly Aames. By allowing herself to get sidetracked into personal conversation and then those kisses, she very well might have jeopardized Jack's willingness to help her.

This wouldn't leave her dead in the water but it would make things awkward.

The memory of his lips touching hers came flooding back as she walked along an aisle lined with cereal boxes, crackers and cookies. She'd been kissed any number of times in her life but never with that intensity, never with that swelling desire that traveled from his heated mouth to hers and back again. Never, ever like Jack Wheeler kissed her, as though theirs was the first and last kiss in the world.

Someone had to use some common sense, right?

Someone had to acknowledge that being intimate was a bad idea.

Or was it?

She liked him. He must like her. She found him irresistible. He must find her the same. What was the harm in mutual attraction, at least from her vantage point?

Ginny made a fuss near the ice cream freezer, so Roxanne let her choose a juice bar. As she watched the little girl struggle with the cellophane wrapper, she understood what the dangers were: obligations. Hers to Grandma Nell. His to Sal. And most importantly—to Ginny.

The child had been excellent at the station. She'd brought along a pink-and-purple backpack full of toys and a lunch that Sal had prepared for her. For the most part, while Roxanne was on the air, Ginny had played with her stuffed bears and eaten watermelon cubes and peanut butter.

"Want help with that wrapper?" she asked.

Ginny shook her head.

"Does everyone at your house like chicken?" Roxanne asked the child as they stopped in front of the meat counter.

"I don't know," Ginny said, still busily trying to unwrap the frozen juice bar.

"Wait a second, you guys had chicken at your birthday party," Roxanne said. Was it really only two days before? It seemed more like two months. However, more to the point, what would she do with a whole chicken? "What about hamburgers? Do you like hamburgers?"

"I like ice cream," Ginny said, finally getting the plastic wrap open. She started licking the frozen treat—her lips were cherry red within seconds.

"Honey, concentrate. How about dinner? Let's see... Pork chops?"

Ginny shrugged.

Roxanne paused as she studied a package of loin chops. Wait a second... What was going on here? What in the world would she do with pork chops? Roxanne went back to the frozen-food section and picked out two large ready-to-bake pizzas.

At the checkout counter, she found an old coffee can wrapped in paper. She picked it up to look at the computer-generated label.

"That's for Tony's parakeets," the clerk said as he to-taled up the pizza and the juice bar.

There were no words on the label, just a picture of an elderly woman holding a cage on her lap, a green-and-yellow parakeet perched on a swing inside.

"What do you mean?" she asked as she wrote a check.

The clerk stared at the Seattle address on the check and scowled. He was a middle-aged man, probably the owner of the store since his name tag read Ben, and the store was called Ben's Shop and Go. It was clear he didn't trust an out-of-state check.

Then he looked closely at Ginny. Glancing back at Roxanne, he smiled broadly. "You must be the gal staying with Doc Wheeler. Roxanne Salyer, right? Hey there, Ginny, is that tasty?"

"Cherry," Ginny said around a mouthful of frozen juice.

He looked back at Roxanne. "I heard you on the radio this morning. Listen, if you don't mind my saying so, you've got to put some animation into the local ads."

"I—I thought I did."

"Well, sure, I guess you tried, but Nancy always makes my store sound...I don't know, fun."

"I'm sorry. I'll try to jazz things up tomorrow."

"Thanks. Starting Wednesday, all the baby food goes on sale. Twenty percent off everything, from strained peaches to teething biscuits."

"Baby food. Figures. Well, I'll do my best."

"That's the spirit. I've got a sale going on suntan lotion right now," he added with a lingering look at Roxanne's peeling nose.

She'd all but forgotten about her sunburn. "Thanks, but I think the worst is over. Have you lived here a long time, Ben?"

"All my life."

She thought he looked younger than forty, but by now it was standard operating practice to say, "Have you ever heard of a woman named Dolly Aames?"

"Never. Why?"

A bell jingled behind her. "Never mind. Say, what did you mean that this can is for Tony's parakeets?"

"To help pay for his project, you know."

"I don't know."

"He raises parakeets," a voice said from behind her.

Jack's voice. Damn, but her heart fluttered!

Roxanne turned abruptly to face him. "When they get old enough," he added as he kissed Ginny on the top of her head and avoided a gooey hug, "Tony uses the money he collects in these cans to buy cages and seed, then he delivers the birds to shut-ins. Once a week, he drives around and makes sure the birds are being cared for. He gave one to your mother-in-law last year, didn't he, Ben?"

Trying hard to ignore the way her body reacted to Jack's proximity—accelerated heartbeat, heightened awareness in every female part of her anatomy—Roxanne said, "Tony does all that? Does he get paid for it? Does he do it through a church or school or something?''

''No.''

''Then what's in it for him?''

The clerk looked at Jack. ''You tell her how it works, Doc.''

Jack turned his full attention on Roxanne; she braced herself by wedging herself between the shopping cart and the counter. He looked urbane and cultured even though his work uniform didn't include a tie and jacket. He also looked so handsome that she mentally chastised herself for drawing away the night before. What was she, crazy?

She was on vacation, right? What was wrong with a little shipboard romance, so to speak? Besides everything, that is.

He smiled benignly, easing a little of her discomfort. ''What's in it for him? Satisfaction, I guess,'' Jack said. ''The kid just likes to help people.''

''That's right,'' Ben added.

Roxanne was impressed. Who would have thought that Tony had this kind of compassion lurking in his seventeen-year-old soul?

Gesturing at the pizza, Jack added, ''Dinner?''

She was immediately embarrassed. She'd offered to fill in at his house and here she was buying frozen pizza. Why hadn't she ever learned to cook? Her mother's idea of putting together a meal was extreme: either she served fruit and yogurt or she called a caterer. Grandma Nell had been a great cook when she was younger.

''Dinner,'' she said, vowing to herself to read a cookbook before bed that night.

Jack followed Roxanne outside. ''I looked out the window and saw my car over here so I figured you were shopping,'' he explained. ''I came right over. I had to see you.''

Despite all her pep talks, her anxiety, her desire to approach this interlude of her life with some measure of self-control, Roxanne's heart leapt at the thought that Jack had been actively looking for her.

"I saw Nancy this morning," he said as he took the keys and the grocery bag from Roxanne, opened his trunk, stowed the groceries and extracted a plastic container of premoistened wipes. As he spoke, he cleaned the red fruit juice off Ginny's hands and face with practiced ease. "She was listening to your radio show."

"Did she say anything?"

"She thought you did great."

"That's a relief," Roxanne said, vaguely disappointed that what he wanted to say to her was so determinedly impersonal. "The man inside the store didn't like the way I read his ad."

"Don't pay too much attention to Ben," he said as he buckled Ginny into her car seat. "Anyway, Nancy is very relieved that you've offered to fill in for a while. She says Teresa will be back in a week or so to take over. And she wants to pay you for your time."

"No," Roxanne said succinctly.

"But—"

"Jack, you tell Nancy that it's a favor, clear and simple. People who live in big cities know how to help other people on occasion, too. Besides, I have an idea for a contest I want to run. Do you think she'll let me?"

"If it isn't indecent or immoral or will alienate her advertisers, I imagine she'll be happy to let you do whatever your heart desires."

"Can I visit her?"

He thought for a second, and nodded. "Why not? I'm sure she's teetering on the edge of boredom already. Have you heard anything about your car?"

"Not a word, but I wasn't at the Cactus Gulch like I told Oz I would be. As the car wasn't parked beside the road when we drove past on our way to the station, I assume Oz towed it back to his place. Ginny and I are going over there right now. With any luck, you can have your car back tomorrow so you won't have to drive your old truck into town."

He smiled in that way he had. "I don't mind driving the old truck."

They stared at each other for a second. She was recalling the feel of his arms around her body, the perfect way she'd seemed to fit in his embrace. His mind, it seemed, was following the same path.

He said, "About last night—"

"Yes?"

"You were right."

"Oh."

"Good thing one of us was thinking."

"You were thinking, too," she said softly.

His eyebrows raised. "What do you mean?"

"I could tell you were distracted."

"So now it's my fault?" he snapped with a challenging gleam in his eyes.

"*What's* your fault?" Roxanne suddenly became aware that several pedestrians had stopped what they were doing and were staring at them. She lowered her voice and added, "I wasn't assigning fault."

Jack looked around him, nodding to people he obviously knew. Grimacing, he said, "We'll talk later." He opened her door and she slid behind the wheel. Without a backward glance he walked across the street toward his office.

Roxanne pulled up in front of Oz's big metal building a few minutes later. The door was rolled up all the way and Roxanne's car was up on a hydraulic lift inside. Oz walked toward her, wiping his hands on a faded pink grease rag. "Tried to reach you," he said succinctly.

"Long story," she said, unbuckling Ginny from her car seat. The little girl looked toward the house, squealed and ran off.

"Ginny!" Roxanne called.

"It's okay," Oz said. "She just sees her great-aunts, that's all." In an aside to Roxanne, he added, "Those two old ladies have more or less taken over Lisa and the twins. Not that I'm complaining," he added.

Roxanne watched as an elderly woman who looked familiar from Ginny's birthday party opened the front door of the tiny house and gathered the child into her plump arms.

"You did a number on your car," Oz said.

Roxanne's attention swung back to Oz. She squeaked, "I did? Good thing I contacted my insurance company."

"Ah, heck, it ain't gonna cost you much to fix it, seeing as you're a friend of Doc's." He proceeded to tell her what she'd done to her car and how he would fix it.

Roxanne said, "Sounds like a plan."

"I hear you're staying out at Doc's."

By now Roxanne wasn't too surprised that her living arrangements were known all over town. She said, "Yes, I'll be there for a few days."

"Right. Say, I heard you on the radio this morning." He looked down at his feet, bit the inside of his cheek and added, "About my ad. This is a garage, you know, not a nightclub. I thought maybe you were just a bit too...hyper."

"Hyper?"

"Nancy is real calm. Makes the garage sound reliable."

Roxanne shook her head. "Okay. I'll tone it down."

"Thanks."

"Roxanne, look!"

Roxanne turned to find Ginny walking toward her, a huge ice cream cone clutched precariously in both hands.

One hundred percent of her concentration was devoted to not tipping the pink ice cream off the cone.

"For you," Ginny said right before she tripped on one of the paving bricks and fell to the ground. The ice cream ended up in a tire planter.

Ginny screeched.

Oz said, "Jeez, that had to hurt."

Roxanne ran to Ginny. Kneeling down, she helped the little girl stand up. "Are you hurt?" she quizzed as she brushed imbedded pebbles from Ginny's dimpled knees. "Are you okay?"

Her questions were met with renewed wails, but they seemed to be focused on the ruined ice cream and not Ginny's minor injuries. She'd scraped her knees and palms—nothing serious, Roxanne knew that, but she still felt like an awful baby-sitter.

"Some mother I'd make," she whispered as she took a tissue out of her pocket and tried to mop Ginny's hand.

"Bring the child on in and we'll fix her up," the older woman beckoned from the doorway. "You must be Jack's friend. I'm his aunt Veronica and this is Sadie, my sister. We're Jack's father's sisters, the old maids in town. Calm down, Ginny. We'll get Roxanne and you both more ice cream. Go with Sadie and get cleaned up. If your father sees you all scratched, he'll have you in surgery." This last comment was met with raucous laughter from both elderly sisters.

Lisa and her twins were nowhere in sight, but the interior of the house had undergone a discernible change. It was still warm despite the twirling overhead fan, and it was still tiny and cluttered, but there was organization to the clutter now. And, more importantly, delicious aromas wafted from the kitchen.

"What's that smell?"

Veronica sniffed and waved impatiently with one hand.

"Chicken stock, going to be chicken soup. Nothing special about it."

"Maybe not to you, but it smells like heaven to me."

"Go on. Really? You don't make chicken stock?"

"I'm not even sure what it is."

Veronica let loose another profound laugh. "Well, I can see Sadie's got her work cut out for her!"

Roxanne wasn't sure what that meant and was even less sure that she wanted to know. She said, "Where are Lisa and the babies?"

Veronica Wheeler was somewhere between sixty and seventy. She was a large woman with a florid complexion, dyed red hair and flamboyant taste in clothes if her current outfit of pink jeans and a turquoise rhinestone-studded blouse were any indication. Her sister, Sadie, had about the same build and seemed to be close in age, but she was obviously cut from different cloth. Her hair was naturally gray, she wore glasses perched on her nose, a light blue dress and sensible shoes.

"We sent Lisa to have her hair washed and cut. The twins are sleeping, or they were before Ginny started carrying on. I hear the beeper, honey, which means the stock needs tending, so you go check on the babies for me, will you? They're in a crib next to their parents' bed."

Roxanne let herself into the darkened bedroom. She found the crib and the babies, one at each end, both on their backs. One was sound asleep and the other was fussing. Roxanne picked up the fretful baby, cradling her in her arms, and perched on the edge of the mattress.

The baby had dark red toenails!

Roxanne carried her to the door where the light was better.

"Midnight Madness," Veronica called from the kitchen doorway. "Sadie painted her toenails so we could tell them apart. That's Sue you're holding."

Smiling, Roxanne returned to the room. She cooed and clucked and made all sorts of other sounds she was heretofore unaware she knew how to make, and pretty soon, Sue settled down and her eyes closed.

What a sweet, tiny package a small baby was. How soft, and how adorable. Roxanne found her lips puckering solely on their own accord, and she kissed the baby's downy head. The child stirred a little, and reluctantly Roxanne put her back in the crib. Somewhere in her chest, she felt her heart constrict and she wasn't sure why.

For some reason, Grandma Nell came to her mind, and with such a rush that it made Roxanne uneasy.

Was there some kind of kismet at work here in Tangent? Had fate brought Roxanne to this town at this time and surrounded her with newborn life in order to remind her that no one lived forever, that old life had to pass on so that new life could take its place?

Did all this have something to do with Grandma Nell's illness, and was Dolly Aames simply the catalyst that conspired to teach Roxanne this one huge lesson of life?

Was that crazy, or what?

She whispered, "I get the point. No one needs to die or anything. I understand."

Jack wasn't sure how it had all come to be, but somehow Roxanne had hooked up with his aunts. Even now, she was in the kitchen with the two old rascals, taking cooking lessons, Ginny hanging on their every move. Of course, after the frozen pizza of two nights before—pizza Roxanne had allowed to thaw before she cooked it—this wasn't all bad.

Sal was sitting in her platform rocker, reading the paper. He hadn't been surprised when she refused to join the other women. It had always seemed to him that Sal didn't get along with his aunts, even though they were all of more or less the same age and were polite to one another. He could recall family gatherings where Sal would disappear into her room rather than interact with his aunts. And it was no secret that she steadfastly avoided Roxanne.

It suddenly occurred to him that this would be an excellent time to talk to her. He tried to think of a way to casually broach the subject of Dolly Aames. He wasn't at all convinced that Sal was evasive when it came to answering questions about this woman—for that matter, Sal was surly when it came to many things. It was just her nature. He thought it more likely she was annoyed with being grilled, and that Roxanne, desperate to help her grandmother, was misreading Sal's reaction. Still, he'd promised Roxanne...

Laughter erupted from the kitchen. Sal looked up from her paper, a flash of irritation crossing her features. "What in the world are they giggling about?"

Good question. What was so all fired funny about learning how to cook a chicken? He said, "I have no idea. Listen, Sal, I'd like to talk to you about something."

"Shoot," she said, folding the paper down on itself and studying him from behind her glasses.

He cleared his throat. Sal was an intensely private woman. His father had told him that repeatedly over the years, hoping to curb a youngster's curiosity and lack of tact. He said, "You know, it occurred to me the other night that I don't know much about you."

Sal fixed him with a stare that, had he been twenty years younger might have sent him scurrying away. He added, "For instance, I know you were born in Idaho, but I don't know a thing about your parents or siblings."

"I was an only child, just like you," she said frostily. "Why are you suddenly interested in my parents?"

"It just seems odd that you don't talk about them."

"It's never seemed odd to you before now," she grumbled.

"Actually, as a matter of fact, it has."

"Your father respected my privacy," she said.

"I know he did. And so do I. I was just thinking about this woman Roxanne is trying to find, this Dolly Aames. I was just wondering if you might not have known her. Years ago, I mean. Maybe you've all but forgotten her…"

His words petered out because she'd suddenly taken off her glasses and was polishing the lenses with the tail of her cotton shirt, something he'd never seen her do before.

"Sal?"

"Why are you doing this?" she mumbled with a swift glance at his face.

The confidence he'd felt all along that Roxanne was barking up the wrong tree and that Sal was just being Sal, faded away. Good heavens, she *was* dodging direct answers.

"Because I care about you. Ever since Roxanne showed up and started asking about Dolly Aames, you've been acting…strange."

"I have not!"

Jack had never divulged his knowledge of the tragedy of Sal's past. Privately, however, he'd wondered if it had been wise for Sal to keep such an important part of her life bottled up inside. Years of caring for people had taught him two things: first, sometimes a good airing did more for the soul than festering secrets. Second, there were times when a man should trust his instincts.

"I know about your past," he said softly.

This earned him an even swifter glance, but the alarm in her eyes stunned him. "Your father promised me he would never tell a soul," she said with a tremor.

"As far as I know, he never did. I looked at your old records last year when you were sick. You'd never been my patient until then, Sal, but you asked me to care for you and I needed to know your medical history."

"So you know…"

"About your husband and your baby and the accident. Yes. I'm so sorry."

"I—I don't like to think or talk about it," she said, carefully replacing her eyeglasses. "It all happened a lifetime ago. I almost didn't survive the loss. Your dad offered me sanctuary. I've never looked back. I don't appreciate your trying to make me think about things best left forgotten."

Now, what in the hell did that mean? As he was trying to figure out his next approach, Roxanne stepped into the living room, her pink cheeks flushed even pinker, her dark eyes sparkling with humor.

Sal, rising swiftly from her chair, used Roxanne's interruption to mumble something about helping to set the table. Roxanne looked after the older woman with a puzzled expression on her face. Then she looked at him, and he forgot, for a while, Sal's idiosyncrasies.

Gazing at Roxanne, Jack realized that she was the kind of woman who looked different every time you looked at her. He wasn't sure how she did it, but she could actually go from pixie to enchantress all within the same conversation. A camera could never capture her—one would need to record her on a videotape. She truly was a woman made for television.

"Dinner is ready," she announced with a flourish and a bow. And then, in a whisper as he passed by her, she added, "What's wrong with Sal?"

"Nothing," he said.

"You haven't been browbeating her, have you?"

"Very funny."

"Just checking. And by the way, your aunts say they've never heard of Dolly Aames."

"Dolly Aames," he said with a sigh. "I'm getting sick of this woman."

George, his aunts' driver, insisted on eating in the kitchen, and Grace was still confined to bed, so Carl took his dinner in to eat with her. As a result, Jack was more outnumbered than usual at the table. The expectant eyes of his two elderly aunts, one whirlwind of a television producer and his three-year-old daughter were all trained on him as he took a bite of chicken covered in a glossy orange sauce. Only Sal nibbled at her dinner and seemed as out of the loop as he was.

"Delicious," he said.

Roxanne beamed. "Sweet-and-sour chicken," she said. "Veronica said it was your mother's recipe."

"Really? I don't remember it."

"Your mother was an excellent cook," Aunt Sadie said.

"Remember her garlic mashed potatoes?" Aunt Veronica added. "Mind you, this was over forty years ago before everyone and their brother put garlic into anything and everything. Hers were so creamy."

"I loved her chocolate cake," Jack said. "She'd make it every year for Christmas, and sometimes when we took picnics up into the hills on horseback."

"I remember that cake," Aunt Sadie said. "Heavenly. I saw the recipe tonight when I was looking through her box."

"My grandmother made a chocolate cake to die for, too," Roxanne said. "She put cherries between the layers. I haven't thought of that cake in years."

"Has your grandmother passed?" Aunt Veronica asked softly.

Jack glanced at Roxanne's face. He wasn't sure if he should jump in and steer the conversation into happier waters, or leave Roxanne to fend for herself. It was his impulse to help her.

He shouldn't have worried. She shook her head, a lovely smile lighting her eyes, and addressed her comment to Sal. "No. She's been ill lately, really ill, and we're all worried about her, but Grandma is a strong woman."

Sal looked up from her plate and Jack saw her and Roxanne exchange a long look.

Aunt Sadie plowed in. "Veronica, why don't we bake one of Jack's mother's chocolate cakes for Roxanne?"

At the same time, more or less, Roxanne said, "Oh, I—"

Jack said, "Now, Aunts—"

And Ginny squealed, "A picnic! Yes! On the horses? Daddy, please, oh please."

"What a nice idea," Aunt Veronica said. "Jack, why don't you? Here Roxanne is on vacation and all you've got her doing is working. It's cruel."

Aunt Sadie added, "And you work too much yourself, young man. When was the last time you had some fun?"

"Last week at Ginny's birthday party," he said.

"You know what I mean. You're too serious. Isn't he, Sal?"

Sal looked up from pushing the rice around on her plate. She shrugged. "Oh, I don't know."

"I do," Aunt Veronica stated. "Jack, you take Roxanne and Ginny up to Sandy Butte. Sadie and I will pack a picnic lunch for you to take along, won't we, Sadie?"

"Absolutely," Sadie said. "How about Saturday?"

"What do you say, Jack?"

Ginny grabbed his arms and pleaded with her blue eyes.

Roxanne said, "You're all forgetting one thing. I don't know how to ride a horse."

The silence this remark created was broken by Aunt Veronica. "Oh, pish-posh," she said. "Jack can teach you. It's an easy trip anyway and he has a couple of well-behaved horses, don't you, Jack?"

"I do, but if Roxanne is nervous about riding—"

"I'd love to learn," she said, meeting his gaze. If anything, she looked more flushed than before. She also looked absolutely breathtaking. "If you don't mind teaching me," she added.

What was he supposed to say? That he didn't want to teach her because it would mean touching her, talking to her, watching her? Every molecule in his body was yearning to do those very things.

"He'd love to teach you," Sadie said.

Just then Roxanne smiled at him and he found himself powerless to resist her. He said, "We'll start tomorrow night."

Chapter Eight

Roxanne caught a glimpse of Jack and Ginny as she bobbed around in a circle atop a previously unseen red horse named Rojo. Ginny straddled the fence railing, watching. Jack stood near his daughter. She could tell, by the way he studied the ground between glances up at her, that he was doing everything in his power not to laugh at her painfully amateur efforts. Even his hat, pulled low, couldn't completely mask the twinkle in his blue eyes.

She couldn't blame him. They'd been out here for an hour and she wasn't getting any better. Her butt hurt. Her elbows flopped so much, she was in danger of launching herself. Worst of all, her breasts jiggled, up and down, every time the horse moved. Despite her bra, despite every effort she made to make them be still, they bounced around like a couple of corks floating on a stormy sea.

"You're getting quite a show," she said as she rounded by Jack again.

He dropped his hand and sure enough, he was grinning. "You're doing better," he said.

"Liar. How do I make this beast stop?"

"Like before."

"I forgot how I did it before," she grumbled.

"Pull back on the reins and say, 'Whoa.'"

She pulled back on the reins. The horse tossed his head, but eventually came to a stop. After taking a much-needed deep breath and thanking her lucky stars that lesson one was over, Roxanne contemplated the next step—dismount. Trouble was, she was sore and shaky and the ground looked a mile and a half away.

Jack put his hand up for the reins, which she was only too glad to give him. He led the horse to the fence and looped the leather straps around a post. As Ginny patted the horse's white blaze, Jack came back by Roxanne's leg and looked up at her.

"Honestly, you did very well."

"Honestly, you are an awful liar. Help me get the heck off this horse."

"Remember how I taught you? Dismount from the near side."

"I don't remember what the near side is."

"The left."

"Okay, but I have to warn you that right now I'm about ready to slide off and take my chances with the ground."

Laughing, he said, "Take your right foot out of the stirrup, swing it over the back of the saddle, take your left foot out, hold on to the back of the saddle and to the horn, and slide to the ground."

She did as directed, hanging in midair for a second before feeling his hands grasp her around the waist and lower her to the ground. She turned to face him. His grip loosened but his hands stayed around her midsection. She looked up into his eyes.

"You're going to make honorary title of cowgirl yet. You just wait and see," he said.

"All this just to get a piece of chocolate cake. I'm shameless."

"But it's an exceptional chocolate cake," he said.

Roxanne felt the urge to stand on her tiptoes and connect with Jack's lips so strongly that it made her head swim.

"You're not done yet," he said softly. "We need to loosen the cinch, take off the saddle and put old Rojo to bed. I'll show you how."

"I'll bet you will," she said.

Sal called for Ginny. Amid protests, the little girl ran inside for her evening bath. Roxanne helped Jack take care of Rojo. As she put the saddle in the barn, he led the horse back to another corral. Roxanne gingerly climbed up the hay on shaky legs, plopped down near the kittens and took a deep, deep breath.

All she wanted was to quiz Sal, find Dolly and go home.

All she wanted was to make passionate love to Jack Wheeler first.

This caused her to smile. The kittens mewed, and she stared down at them. They'd changed so much in five short days.

Five days. Her own life seemed half a world away instead of a few hundred miles. The radio station in Tangent seemed more real than the television station in Seattle. All this in just five days?

Things were going much too fast.

She carefully picked up the white kitten and ran her finger over his fuzzy ears. She was in a time warp.

"Are you in here?" Jack called from the door.

"No one here but me and the cats and the dogs and the horses," she said.

Goldy whinnied at the sound of Jack's voice. Roxanne watched as he ran a hand along her jaw. He fetched her a bucket of grain before patting the foal who was now named Poco Oro, or Little Gold. He stopped for a few words with

Aggie and her pups, then he effortlessly climbed up the bales and sat down next to Roxanne.

"I see you've gotten over your hesitation about holding kittens," he said, touching the animal's nose.

"Yeah, I guess I have. This one must be Casper."

"I assume. By the way, I heard you mention your contest on the radio this morning. I was over at the hospital, checking on Nancy."

"What did she think of it?"

"She thought it was inspired."

"I was hoping she'd like it. She gave me the go-ahead, but you always wonder."

"Rest assured. Where did you come up with the idea for a contest about local do-gooders?"

Shrugging, Roxanne said, "I've always been interested in people who make a difference. My boss in Seattle isn't quite so excited about the idea, says it's passé. I don't think so. Anyway, I talked some of the downtown merchants into donating small gifts. Now all we need is community support and a few nominees."

"Who's going to choose the winners?"

"Nancy. Paul will take the nominations in to her on Thursday evening, then I'll announce the big winner on Friday. This way, she gets to keep her hand in things and I thought it might help her pass the time."

"Good thinking," he said slowly, his eyes glued to her face.

The way he looked at her was absolutely exhilarating. It made her feel desirable and beautiful and special. How he did it, she wasn't sure, but the look in his eyes was enough to unravel her.

"I have to admit I'm partial to Tony as our first winner," she said. "I think what he's doing with the parakeets is not only good-hearted but really original."

"I agree," he said, his gaze unwavering.

"However, a woman called in today about a man out on the highway who stopped and helped two elderly people when their car broke down. That story has a soft spot in my heart because I went through the same thing. But you came along—"

"I do not want to be nominated as a local hero," Jack said, his brow creasing.

He looked very beguiling when he frowned that way. It was all she could do not to lean forward and kiss him.

"Anyway," she added, "I'm anxious to see what calls and letters we get over the next few days."

"And pretty soon you'll be gone," Jack said, looking away at last.

Roxanne hadn't thought of it that way, but of course he was right. She said, "I'll brief Teresa when she gets back. Hopefully she'll keep it up." Roxanne put the kitten back with its siblings, and faced Jack. "Have you had a chance to talk to Sal?"

"A little."

"A little?"

"A thing like this takes finesse, Roxanne. I'm setting the groundwork. How about your grandmother? Have you talked to her lately?"

"Two days ago. She was coughing—I'll call her again this weekend. I was hoping to have something positive to tell her."

"You said I could have nine days," he said.

"I know. I'm sorry I brought it up."

"You're understandably anxious," he said, putting his hand on hers where it rested on the hay.

She stared at their fingers—his, larger, darker, stronger. She could feel the heat of his hand all the way up her arm and down into her groin. She wanted him to hold her, to kiss her.

She said, "I guess we'd better be off to bed."

His voice dropped to a husky whisper as he said, "Do you mean that the way I hope you mean it or the way I'm pretty sure you mean it?"

Their eyes met again and a shiver of recognition tingled Roxanne's spine. The answer didn't trip off her tongue as fast as it should have. The delay spun his playful remark into new realms of possibilities.

He raised her hand to his lips, kissed her fingers, and she closed her eyes. She was afraid to look at him, sure that if she saw the same passion in his face that she felt building in her body that she would forfeit all control.

He kissed her hand again, mumbled her name. Opening her eyes, she found him staring at her face as though memorizing her features, the same way she longed to study him. She wanted to commit every detail of him to memory.

"I know we shouldn't," he said softly.

"Let's anyway," she replied as she leaned forward and touched her lips to his.

Roxanne gave in to a sense of destiny as the world shrank to the connection between the two of them. She opened her mouth, felt his tongue slide against hers, felt the results of this all the way into the center of her being. He kissed her eyelids, her neck, his lips warm and moist. She licked his ear. It was as though they were using their mouths to test, to taste, to *know*.

But in the end, their kisses created more stress than relief.

"I don't know what to do about you," Jack whispered, his lips moving against her cheek.

"Jack—"

"I mean it. I make resolutions, then I hurry to break them. I decide you don't want a thing to do with me so I don't want a thing to do with you—"

"That's not true," she interrupted. How could he be so far off base?

"You have me so confused, Roxanne."

"The feeling is entirely mutual," she told him.

He kissed her lips again and she yearned to jump into his arms, the world be damned.

"Off to bed then," he added. He didn't need to add the word *alone*. It was understood.

By Thursday, Roxanne had four nominees for the local hero of the week. By Friday morning, Nancy Kaufman had sent her husband, Paul, into the station with the winner's name sealed in an envelope. Tony and his parakeets didn't win, nor did the man on the highway. Nancy chose as winner a handicapped boy who had trained all year to run in the Special Olympics, then had to bow out because his mother fell ill and he refused to leave her with strangers. He might have missed winning a trophy then, but thanks to the largesse of the jewelry store downtown, he had one now.

By Saturday morning, Sadie and Veronica had delivered a picnic packed very carefully into a small cooler that Jack tied onto the back of his horse. With most everyone looking on, Roxanne managed to swing herself up into the saddle and follow Jack out of the yard and onto the trail without a major mishap. Between one thing and another, her riding lessons had begun and ended on the same day, thank goodness. Now she could plod along behind Jack and Ginny without an audience.

The big red horse seemed bored with the route, which was okay with Roxanne. Ahead of her, she could hear the deep rumble of Jack's voice and Ginny's bubbly laughter. Jack was holding Ginny on the saddle in front of him, and the two of them talked and sang and carried on. Roxanne used all available energy and concentration to stay on the horse.

Out in the desert, the animal's rolling gait reminded Roxanne of a ship at sea. Even the creaking of the leather sounded like a boat. Sometimes he stumbled on a rock and did a little dip thing that caused Roxanne's heart to plummet into her shoes, but mostly he plodded, clip-clop, his footfalls thudding against the hard-packed trail. Roxanne's gaze wavered between the scenery and the sight of Jack perched on a saddle. Honestly, she was hopeless.

It was a beautiful, if hot, day. The sky was a light aqua blue, filled with stringy clouds that mitigated the effect of the sun and teased a person into thinking there might be rain on the way. The desert itself was as huge and peaceful as ever. Take away a few distant power and telephone poles, and the horizon looked as it must have for centuries.

Eventually the trail started to rise. Roxanne held on to the horn of the saddle and a hank of Rojo's reddish mane, leaning forward to offer encouragement. Rojo had no trouble making his way up the trail. He found sure footing on the uneven terrain and she grew to trust his steady get-the-job-done walk.

The hillside was deceptive. Just when Roxanne figured they had to be at the top of the bluff, there was another twist and another rise. Brush gave way to stunted trees, the temperature began to cool down. Rojo good-naturedly shuffled along. Roxanne began obsessing about the ride down.

Finally the bluff leveled off. Roxanne loosened her grip on the horse and looked for Jack.

He'd made it up far before her and was waiting in the shade of a small tree, he and Ginny still astride Milo. He watched her approach with amusement and something else flashing in his eyes. She loved him in that disreputable hat. She couldn't believe how much he changed—from doctor to rancher—just by putting that hat on his head.

"Your elbows aren't waving around as much," Jack said as she drew up beside him.

"Ah, flattery. My rear is killing me."

Laughing, he gestured at her canteen. "Be sure to take a drink from that every once in a while."

"I do. I'm hoping we're at the end of the line."

"Almost. Aren't we, Ginny?"

Ginny was busily gnawing on an apple, but she nodded.

"The view from up here is splendid," Roxanne said, peering out from beneath the brim of her cap. She found it hard to believe she'd been stranded in countryside almost as desolate just a week before. "There must be a hundred shades of brown," she said. "It doesn't look as though anything could live out there."

"You'd be surprised," Jack said. "Those little green spots out there are mesquite groves. If you were to nose around in them, you'd find all sorts of signs of habitation— from old tin cans miners left, to pack rats' nests to animal tracks. There are rabbits, kit fox, snakes, lizards and even coyote. What you're looking toward is Death Valley."

"Which I recall from school is the hottest and driest spot in the United States."

"Named by a stranded forty-niner," Jack added. "But the Native Americans had another name for it. Tomesha, Ground Afire."

"It fits."

"We're going up just a little bit higher, to those trees."

Within another few minutes, they'd reached their destination. As Ginny scrambled up a shaded rock and unpacked her ever-present bag of stuffed bears, Jack helped Roxanne off her horse. His hands didn't linger this time.

"It's all so different from Seattle," Roxanne said, moving closer to the bluff, distancing herself a little from Jack.

"No water to speak of," he said succinctly as he loosened the cinches on their saddles and tethered the horses.

"No surplus water, no boats, no fluffy white clouds, no seagulls. It's like a whole other world. I wish I could show you Seattle." The words were out before she could think about the wisdom of saying them. Jack didn't even look at her. He was unlashing the picnic cooler.

"I've seen your neck of the woods," he said at last, spreading a blanket out beneath the tree. "During summer break one year I traveled up the West Coast, then across to Vancouver, Canada, then back here. It's beautiful up there. Kind of wet, though."

"Yes," she said, suddenly wistful. Perhaps she was homesick.

Roxanne looked off the bluff at the barren land before her. Sand, rocks and little trees. Dusty brown, tan, ivory, greens so muted they almost didn't exist. The sky was pale. It stunned her that just a few days before, she'd tackled the desert with so little preparation.

"I got claustrophobic in Seattle," Jack said. He'd come up behind her and stood slightly to her left. His proximity surprised and pleased her. She was constantly finding herself in the same conundrum he'd confessed to being in a couple of nights before—telling herself one thing, feeling another.

"I don't understand what you mean," she said.

"There are so many trees and buildings and mountains where you live that your line of vision is always interrupted. Add the fog and the clouds and the rain pressing down from above and the world seems...well, small."

"Not here, though," Roxanne said. "The world seems enormous here." She turned to face him. "Coming here like this must make you kind of sad, Jack."

Frowning, he said, "Now why would you say that?"

"I know you used to come here a lot. Your aunts told me. I don't know much about your ex-wife, but—"

"Now, wait a second," he said holding up a hand. "I never came here with Nicole."

Roxanne stared at him openmouthed.

"Nicole hated horses, deserts, picnics, rocks, snakes, buzzards, sand, me—"

Roxanne laughed. "I get the picture." Softly she added, "I'm sure she didn't hate you, Jack. I don't see how she could have hated you."

He swallowed hard, his gaze traveling from her to Ginny, who was still playing on the rock, and back again. "When you say things like that, Roxanne, it makes me...well—"

"I mean it," she said, interrupting because he was obviously having trouble finding the right word.

"I know you do. That's what undoes me. Anyway, maybe you're right. Maybe *hate* isn't the right word. She felt as though I let her down. She counted on me to make her life interesting and fun and different, and look what I offered her."

With this, he spread his arms and it was all Roxanne could do not to fling herself into his embrace. She said, "It wasn't up to you to give her all the things she lacked, Jack. And once she had Ginny—"

"She wanted a baby," he said. "I knew the marriage wasn't good, but when she got pregnant, I was thrilled. I thought that surely a baby would provide the cement that our marriage needed, and besides, I'd always wanted children. I couldn't have been more wrong. For one thing, a baby isn't put on Earth to cement anything, I know that now. It's not a child's place to provide, it's a parent's place.

"Beyond that, however, I failed to take into account Nicole's basic nature. Having a baby to her was like organizing a benefit or hiring a new designer—something different to do. I was thinking family and she was thinking hobby. But like all her other hobbies, Ginny wasn't enough to hold Nicole's attention for long. She got bored."

"What a fool," Roxanne said vehemently.

"We were both fools."

"But she left her daughter."

"Yes. But what if she'd taken Ginny with her? I would have moved heaven and earth to get Ginny back. In some ways, I guess, Nicole actually thought of someone else besides herself when she left Ginny where she was happy, loved and taken care of."

Roxanne thought to herself, *She left Ginny where she wouldn't get in the way of her mother's new romance.* But if Jack wanted to look at it another way, who was she to interfere?

Jack sighed. "So now Ginny has no mother. That's what I feel the worst about. That's why Sal is so important, and even Grace in her own way. But Grace will have a family of her own pretty soon, and she and Carl will want to get their own place. Maybe I'll rebuild the studio for them. They'll be close by because Carl runs the ranch, but it won't be the same. So that means Sal is the female thread of continuity in our home, just as she was for me, just as your grandmother is for you."

Roxanne knew he was telling her that he wasn't going to push Sal anymore, and for the first time, she realized that asking him to do so was unfair. Why should he put himself out for her? More importantly perhaps, why should he jeopardize the peace of mind of a woman he cared about for one who would disappear in a week?

Roxanne made a private vow to herself—she would wait until Jack failed to elicit any information about Sal, and then ask the woman to stop equivocating and just explain herself. Judging from their last conversation, Grandma Nell was the key—Roxanne would bet her job that Sal was concerned about her grandmother. In what capacity, she wasn't sure. Perhaps Dolly Aames had mentioned the nice woman in Washington who was once her friend.

A thought occurred to Roxanne so suddenly that she almost blurted it out loud. What if Sal was really Dolly Aames, hiding her true identity for some unknown reason?

No.

Why not?

It was possible. She tried to merge the photo of Dolly taken out by the longhorn skulls with the wrinkled face of Jack's former nanny, but time's erosion worked against a comparison. The most she could say was that it was *possible* they were the same woman. Sal tended to wear high necklines but if Roxanne could see a dark mole on her neck, then she'd know. If she was really Dolly, then it would explain her touchiness.

But why? Why would she hide out under an assumed name? Why would she lie about her identity?

It didn't matter—not now. What mattered was that Roxanne not put Jack in the middle. After she was gone, if Sal was upset, it should be with her, not Jack.

Gone. In a week. Eventually one of the women at Ginny's party, whom Roxanne had seen eyeing the handsome bachelor daddy, would make her move and Jack would fall in love again.

That thought depressed the heck out of her. She grumbled, "Maybe you'll remarry."

"I make a lousy husband," he said, gently poking her in the ribs. "Maybe it's my taste in women."

She glanced back at him and found a smile on his face. He was obviously teasing her. She shook her head, her thoughts elsewhere. "Jack, does Sal have a mole on her neck, right side?"

"No," he said, shaking his head. "Why do you ask?"

Ginny saved Roxanne answering. "I'm hungry!" she wailed. She'd moved from the rock to the blanket and had the cooler half open.

"I guess it's time to eat," Jack said, and taking Roxanne's hand in a gesture so uncomplicated, it made her eyes sting, led her to the blanket and their picnic. As they ate cold chicken and salads, Roxanne discovered what it was like to be with a real family, small as it was. The cake was just as delicious as promised, but twice as messy. They took turns with a damp cloth, cleaning their faces and hands, helping each other de-chocolate.

When Ginny brought out her bears, Jack surprised Roxanne by lying back on the blanket. He closed his eyes, seemingly at ease, and she stared at him.

One thought kept tumbling through her mind as she fought the desire to touch him. Was this as close to feeling part of a family as she was ever going to get?

That was up to her, wasn't it? She still didn't know for sure where she fit into the great scheme of things, but she realized the power to choose was hers and hers alone.

Gazing down at his strong features made her feel good. Really good. She wanted more—a lot more—and if it had to be temporary, and if it led to loss, then so be it. Roxanne wanted to belong to Jack if even for an hour because the thought of going through the rest of her life without having made the effort suddenly seemed totally unacceptable.

She reached out and smoothed a lock of hair away from his forehead. He opened his eyes and caught her hand. With a sense of destiny, she leaned far over until their lips met.

The ride home seemed twice as long as the ride up into the hills. Despite a nearly perfect day, Jack had felt a kind of heaviness inside for hours now. At first, he'd thought it might have to do with remembering Nicole, talking about her and what went wrong with their marriage. It wasn't until he'd kissed Roxanne that he'd realized it had nothing at all to do with Nicole and everything to do with Roxanne.

This was the way it should have been, he'd thought with a leaden pang. *This is what Ginny deserves. It's what I dreamed marriage was all about.*

The realization had delighted him for a second, but the

feeling didn't—couldn't—last. Roxanne was going to leave in a few days.

A frighteningly big chunk of him wanted to throw caution to the wind and see if she was willing to do the same. He found himself speculating about long-distance relationships, but he was old enough and wise enough to know it would never work. Relationships needed time and energy and focus. He didn't want to enter into one where half the relationship wasn't willing or able to give their fair share. He'd been there before.

So that crossed out a long-distance romance. It was a sure thing that he wasn't moving his family to Washington State, and he couldn't see a woman like Roxanne being happy in a place like Tangent, so there went slow and steady dating. What was left for them?

Nothing.

Or a torrid love affair of short duration.

Personally he was in favor of the torrid love affair, heavy on the torrid part. He could hardly stand looking at her anymore, he wanted to be with her so badly. Touching her was torture. When she looked at him, it started his stomach boiling.

So why not? He had a feeling she was as ripe for romance as he was. He decided he would ask her what she thought. It was no good trying to be clever with a modern woman—better to lay your cards out on the table. Maybe they could make love morning, noon and night for the next week and burn each other right out of their systems.

Yeah, right.

But he had to do something. He couldn't go on with things the way they were.

That night, after returning a few calls gathered from his day's absence, Jack sat in his favorite chair, staring into the aquarium, Ginny on his lap looking at a picture book. His thoughts flittered from an old friend of his father's who was experiencing high-blood pressure and refused to take his medication, to a younger patient's chronic sinus infections.

Ginny pointed at a picture and said, "What's this, Daddy?"

"An armadillo," he told her.

Sal had insisted on giving Ginny a bath after their ride. While she did that, Roxanne had made tacos, which didn't turn out half bad considering everything. Even Grace admitted Roxanne's culinary skills were improving, though he imagined part of her enthusiasm had to do with the long evening visits she and Roxanne had on a nightly basis. The two younger women were slowly becoming friends.

Even now, over the hum of the aquarium and the creaking of Sal's platform rocker, he could hear the lilt of women's laughter. It was a sound that had been muted, maybe even absent over the past two years. It was a sound he found himself enjoying.

Eventually Roxanne appeared in the living room. She'd showered after dinner and had changed into a sleeveless light blue dress with tiny little straps over her creamy shoulders. It was long and straight, probably shapeless when it wasn't hugging every one of her modest but tantalizing curves. The way it slithered when she walked was enough to make his throat constrict. Her hair was loose on her shoulders and most of the burn had faded and blended with a newly acquired tan. He could hardly take his eyes off her.

"Grace is anxious to get back into the kitchen," she said as she sank down on the sofa opposite him, folding her long legs under her. He felt like fanning his face.

"Another week, then we'll see," he said gruffly. "The spotting has stopped."

"She's tired of lying there. I imagine she's also sick of my cooking."

"I thought the tacos were great," he said.

Sal looked up from her book, peered at Roxanne over the top of her glasses and said, "Humph."

Roxanne smiled. She apparently understood Sal's grumble. He didn't. There was no peace when these two women were in the same room.

But that wouldn't be a problem pretty soon, would it?

Sal put down her book. "Come on, Ginny," she said, putting her hand out. "It's time to tuck you into bed."

"But—"

"No buts," Jack said, kissing Ginny's damp hair. "Go with Sal. I'll be in to see you later."

As Ginny climbed off his lap, Sal added, "I'll say good-night now, too." Ginny ran over to Roxanne and hugged her. Roxanne looked surprised by the gesture—and very pleased. She kissed Ginny's forehead. Sal took Ginny's hand in hers and the two of them disappeared down the hall.

"Sal couldn't wait to get away from me," Roxanne whispered. "But I did get a glimpse of her neck earlier and you're right—no mole."

"Told you," he said. "Why did you think she had a mole?"

"Dolly Aames had a mole."

He shook his head. "Honestly, that imagination of yours is really something."

She shrugged. "I had a wonderful day, Jack."

"I did, too." He was nervous. He wanted to talk to her, but the living room seemed a terrible place. He considered his options. There was the barn, the scene of most of their conversations, or the courtyard, which was undoubtedly romantic. The courtyard, he decided, wondering how to lure her out there so he could try to explain, try to understand what was happening between them.

She said, "Grace told me you have birds in your office."

"Finches," he said.

"May I see them?"

"Now?"

"Yes, now," she said, smiling sweetly. It was almost as though she knew what he had planned. That was impossible, though. He said, "Sure. Of course."

She followed him down the hall and he opened the door to his home office. He kept the lights dimmed so as not to shock the birds who were in a large cage in one protected corner of the room.

Turning up the lights a little, he was aware that she'd closed the door behind them. "What a lovely room," she murmured, looking around.

He'd been in this room so many times over the years that he'd stopped seeing it. Now, watching her take in the dark brown leather furniture, the wall of books, the oversize plank made into a desk, the older-than-time Oriental rug and the French doors leading out onto the far end of the courtyard, he had to agree. He said, "My father did most of it. All I've added is the computer and the birds and a few dozen books."

"I can't believe all the books," she said, running her hand over the spines.

"The bottom three shelves are family picture albums," he said, "so don't be too impressed."

"May I look at them?"

"Now?"

"No, silly. Sometime."

"Of course. You're welcome in here anytime you want. But these are old albums. The new ones that include Ginny are in the living room."

They stared at each other for a few seconds, then the

birds chirped. He walked to the corner, aware that Roxanne was close on his heels, and stopped in front of a broad bird cage complete with varying-size branches for perching. His two cinnamon-and-white finches peeped and flitted side to side, hopping on their tiny feet.

"Aren't they cute?" she said, peering into the cage. "What are their names?"

"Myrna and Loy. Myrna is the female, Loy is the male."

"Where are their babies?"

"They're between families," he said. "Now why, Roxanne, did you expect babies?"

"Are you serious?" She smiled at him in a way that made his heart feel like a bowl of tossed greens. "I've seen and heard about nothing but babies in this town."

"Well, like I said, they're between families."

"Which is the male? They both look alike."

"Not to each other," he said dryly.

"Honestly, Jack. How do you tell the female finch from the male?"

Why were they talking about birds? That's what he wanted to know. He said, "The male builds the nests, sings to the female, hops around with bits of grass in his beak, puffs out his feathers. The female just sits there and looks bored with it all."

"She's not bored," Roxanne said, straightening up and turning to face him.

"She's not?"

"Oh, no. She's flattered and amused, that's all."

He looked down into her eyes. It was like falling into a bottomless well at midnight. He said, "So suddenly you're a bird expert?"

"No, but I am a female."

Was she ever.

The room was getting very stuffy. And it was too dark, despite the lights. He moved stiffly to his desk, switched on the lamp and sat down in the swivel chair. It felt good to have a little distance.

What was he thinking? A moment before, he'd wanted her alone, he'd wanted to propose an affair. But here she was talking about mating birds and strutting males and her being female, moving closer to him, pinning him with her dark eyes, and he was running off to the safety of the chair behind his desk.

Actions speak louder than words, he decided, even if the words never made it out of his mouth. He'd had plans, but he'd abandoned them at the first sign of closeness. Obviously his head was glued on straight even if the rest of him was askew.

As she moved toward him again, her dress slid over her gently swaying hips and hugged the luscious curves of her breasts, her stomach, her thighs. It made a silky rustling noise though it was hard to hear because his heart was pounding like a demented drummer, right in his ears. Looking down at him, she pulled the cord on the lamp.

He said, "Roxanne—"

"Too much light for the birds," she said softly, moving so close he had to lean back in his chair to look up at her. "Okay if I sit down?"

He started to say, "Sure, there's a chair right on the other side of the desk," but that wasn't what she had in mind. Without waiting for his response, she sank down onto his lap.

"Put your arms around me," she whispered.

He did as she asked. He felt her body tremble. The realization that she was as nervous as he was made him laugh softly. He said, "Roxanne, I do believe you're trying to seduce me."

"What makes you think that?" she asked, kissing his forehead. This put her breasts close to his face. The soft warmth was like an invitation, and he fought the impulse to tear away the cloth that covered her and claim her right then and there.

"You're playing with fire," he warned as her proximity and her intentions aroused every male particle of his body.

She leaned down, her fragrant hair cascading around his face, and whispered in his ear, "Show me."

Suddenly he didn't feel like laughing. Suddenly, showing her how he felt seemed like one hell of a good idea.

He kissed her, probably too hard, he thought, but he couldn't help it. Her mouth was soft and succulent. He slid his tongue against hers and felt it right down in his groin.

And she kissed him back just as lustily. He tightened his grasp around her body. Her bosom pressed against his arms, his chest; her heartbeat throbbed in her throat. He ran his hands up and down her body, massaging her breasts and legs through the fragile fabric of her dress. Her groans drove him mad as he gathered her closer to him while their kisses grew deeper and longer and wetter, and it was all he could do to remember to breathe, to remember to pump blood to his brain.

She drew away from him, licking her lips. "I've wanted to do that again, ever since the other night," she said softly.

"I've wanted it, too," he told her, drawing her back, kissing her again, teasing her lips open. Her fingers ran through his hair, caressed the back of his neck, splayed across his shoulders. As close as he pulled her, she pressed herself closer still. He ran a hand up her bare leg, under her dress, up her silken thigh. He felt the wispy fabric of her panties. The searing desire to strip them away made him feel faint.

They were close to a point of no return and he knew it. He was having trouble concentrating on anything but immediate gratification. While her nipples were pebbles, the rest of her body seemed to be growing softer, fuller. He wanted to take her out of her clothes, look at every inch of her nude body, kiss her from her hair to her toes, make love to her, right here in the chair, on the desk, on the floor. Anywhere. Everywhere.

Grasping her behind the knees and around the back, he lifted her. She regarded him with deep eyes and murmured, "Where are we going, Jack?" Her voice was thick, her eyes like melted dark chocolate.

"Do you care?"

"No."

"Not here," he said.

"No."

As he walked toward the door, she kissed his neck and licked his ear. His knees felt weak. Her hands ran under his shirt and the feel of her skin, even her hands, against his bare flesh made him shudder. His mind didn't start working again until they were at the door.

How were they to exit this room with lust and longing plastered over every disheveled aspect of their being? What if Carl was walking down the hall right this minute to discuss the livestock auction next month? What if Sal saw his light on and assumed he was alone or making patient calls and was coming to talk to him about Ginny? And what about Ginny? What if she had grown tired of waiting for him to come kiss her good-night? What if she was on the other side of this blasted door?

He looked down at Roxanne, the most alluring woman he'd ever seen, let alone held, and knew he couldn't go through that door, not like this, not at his house, not now. The disappointment he felt just about killed him. He carefully set her down on her feet. A sense of loss swamped him.

"I can't," he whispered.

She looked confused. "You don't want to? I thought—"

He stilled her lips with a fingertip. "No, darling, no. Of course I want to. I'm dying to. I'm going to lie awake for hours tonight wishing I'd kept walking through that door and taken my chances with all the what-ifs. But I'm a family man and this is my family's home. It's early still, and the chances that one or more of them might find us—"

She kissed his fingertip. "A locked door?"

"A locked door would be like setting off fireworks. I'm sorry."

"I am, too," she said. Then smiling wistfully, she added, "I understand."

"I don't see how you can," he muttered.

"Maybe a week ago, I wouldn't have, but after being here for a while, I can see how close you all are, how you look after one another."

"You mean we're all a bunch of busybodies."

Another smile. "I guess. But it's rather sweet. If we want to…well, you know, then we need to find a place that's private. Intimacy isn't a shared family activity."

"This stinks," he said.

She put her arms around him, resting her cheek against his chest. He folded her in an embrace and they stood like that. It was a hard way to calm down, but it was comforting, too. Her body was warm and vibrant, her pulse seemed to synchronize with his own. It gradually occurred to Jack that having sex with Roxanne—while still the fabric of dreams—would never be enough.

He didn't have the slightest idea what to do about it.

Chapter Nine

Two days later, Roxanne walked into the jewelry store. She'd left Ginny at a playmate's house that morning and was aware that she was due to pick her up in less than half an hour.

For two days now, she'd been running around in a daze. Jack had had another emergency with an ailing patient on Sunday so he was gone most of the day, which spared her having to face him after Saturday night's fiasco. On the other hand, it also deprived her of seeing him.

She'd spent Sunday morning at the radio station, the afternoon with Ginny, occasionally attempting to corner Sal in order to ask a few indirect questions, aware that time was passing. But Sal was as slippery as mud at low tide. Add to that the fact that Grandma Nell's doctor had left town, meaning there was no one for the X rays to be delivered to, and it was no wonder Roxanne felt jittery.

The woman behind the counter was older than the brunette who had volunteered the trophy. The brunette, true to form for this town in any female between the ages of twenty and forty, had been pregnant. Roxanne introduced herself, explaining that she represented the radio station.

Nodding vigorously, she said, "I'll get it for you."

She emerged from the back room a few minutes later with a trophy, on the base of which was engraved the winner's name. "My name is Pansy Miller," she said. "I'm filling in for my granddaughter for a week or so. Her baby is due in a couple of months and she and the hubby wanted to take a little vacation, just the two of them."

"Then you're new to town."

"Oh, no. I lived here years ago, ran this store, as a matter of fact, along with my first husband, Bill. We owned that big blue house one block over. Sometimes we rented out rooms. What do you think of the trophy?"

"The trophy looks great. Nancy Kaufman told me to tell everyone here how much she appreciates the donation." As Pansy wrapped it, Roxanne added, "Did you by any chance live here in the early sixties?"

"I lived here until 1966 when I married Ned and moved to Texas. He's my second husband. Bill died in 1964, the same year Mother passed away. What a dreadful year that was."

"I can imagine. I don't suppose you ever heard of a woman named Dolly Aames?" She'd asked the question so many times with so little result that it took her a second to realize that Pansy was struggling with a memory.

"Dolly Aames. I *do* know that name. My mother was named Dolly, you see, and it's kind of unusual. Let's see."

"You knew her?" Roxanne was already imagining the call to her grandmother. *I have another lead,* she'd say. *Hang in there.* And then she'd have to pack her bags and say goodbye to Jack—she couldn't bear to think about this part of success. Success meant leaving early....

"No, honey, I didn't know her," Pansy said. "It was the oddest thing. One winter we got a call from a man asking for Dolly Aames. Said he was her cousin, but wouldn't leave a message. The man called back every night for the better part of a week. We had a couple of guests at the time, an engineer working on a highway project and a sickly young woman, but no one by that name, so it was all kind of odd. It was around Christmas, I remember that. And it must have been 1963 because Mother, Bill and I all talked about it and neither one of them lived to see Christmas 1964.''

''The year is right,'' Roxanne mused as she thought about the postmark on Dolly's letter to Grandma Nell. ''You never heard the name again? Nobody by that name ever showed up?''

''No. I'm sorry, dear. I can tell by your face that you were hoping for more.''

''This is as close to a solid lead as I've come, Pansy, so don't feel bad. I have a little girl to pick up, so I guess I'd better be on my way.''

''Does your daughter look like you or her father?'' Pansy called as Roxanne turned to leave.

''Oh, she's—''

''I bet your husband says she looks like you. You're pretty as a picture, dear.''

Why didn't I correct her? Roxanne asked herself as she closed the door behind her.

But she knew why and it embarrassed her. For one moment, a stranger had thought she was someone's mother—Ginny's mother—and it had felt wonderful. For one moment, a stranger had mentioned her husband, and Jack's face had popped into her mind, and she'd felt her spirits soar right into the stratosphere.

A shiny coin on the sidewalk caught her eye, and Roxanne picked it up, pocketing it for Ginny. Then she took it out again and stared at it.

A found penny. A wish waiting to happen. A wish for

Grandma Nell to be okay. A wish to see Ginny grow. A wish to never say goodbye to Jack.

What did that mean, never say goodbye? Of course she would say goodbye. No matter how they resolved the issue of their mutual lust, there was an inherent sadness built into the equation. She had a job and a life in Seattle, and he had the same things here. There *would* be a goodbye.

And it suddenly dawned on her that if she allowed herself and Jack to give in to their mutual craving for each other, that parting would be twice as devastating.

And yet she ached for him, she yearned for him.

She stared at the penny for what seemed like ages, almost unaware of the passersby who walked around her, of the curious looks thrown her way through shop windows. Something was swelling in her chest, surging up her throat. Her eyes suddenly ached, the back of her nose felt pinched, she trembled like a solitary blade of grass before a great gust of wind. Then, just as quickly, all these sensations ceased.

Grandma Nell always called an intuitive moment an epiphany and until that second, Roxanne had never really understood the impact of one. But she did now.

The foundation for everything in the world that she wanted was right here in this town, right inside the clinic down the street.

Her head snapped up and she looked in that direction. *She was in love with Jack Wheeler.*

Somehow Roxanne made it to her car. Her hands and knees shook.

That's why she'd tried to seduce him, *that's* why looking at him made her pulse hammer and skip, *that's* why she was secretly relieved that Pansy Miller hadn't known exactly where Dolly Aames was, necessitating Roxanne leaving immediately.

Not simple lust—would that it be so! Lust was easily dealt with. But love...

Jack might want her body for a passionate tryst, but love? Hadn't he made it clear that he was through with love? Hadn't he joked around that he was finished with marriage because he fell for the wrong kind of woman...a woman like her mother.

But I'm not like my mother, she thought to herself as tears of wonder cascaded down her cheeks. For the first time, she understood, *she knew.*

I'm nothing like my mother....

A few hours later, she was sitting on the luxurious Oriental carpet that covered the floor in Jack's study because she could think of no way to be closer to him when he wasn't home than to be in this room where she'd spent the most passionate few minutes of her life two days earlier.

Ginny sat cross-legged on the floor. Between the two of them, they had a stack of photograph albums. Roxanne wanted to absorb every detail of Jack's life, his parents' life, his grandparents...

The albums were exceptionally organized and clearly labeled. While Roxanne studied the faces of Jack's great-grandparents, Ginny thumbed through an album marked Easter. In one fist she clutched the new penny Roxanne had given her.

"Look, Daddy had a baby bunny," Ginny said around a mouthful of grapes. "I want a baby bunny, too."

"You don't have a bunny?"

"No. Daddy says people just get them for Easter time and then don't want them. Not me. I want a mommy bunny and a daddy bunny."

"Now you want two bunnies," Roxanne said with a smile.

"That's how you get baby bunnies," Ginny said knowingly.

Roxanne decided to let this subject drop. She said, "Let me see that picture of your daddy."

Ginny turned the album and Roxanne peered at a photo of Jack labeled, Easter Day, 1966. He looked about three years old and he was absolutely adorable. He had the same sparkly blue eyes, but his hair was lighter and finer, like Ginny's. His smile, if nothing else, gave him away—it was the same smile Roxanne adored now. Sure enough, Jack as a toddler had had a white bunny with a pink nose.

Behind Jack, with her slender hands resting on his shoulders, stood a woman in her mid-thirties, with snapping dark eyes, full lips, ebony clouds of wavy hair. "Grandma," Ginny said, pointing at her.

"Really?"

"Daddy told me." Pointing at an obscure figure in the background, she added, "That's Sal. But she was little then. Not as little as me."

Roxanne stared at the younger woman. She'd have to take Ginny's word for it that this was Sal. The twenty-something looked burdened, somehow, preoccupied even though the picture of her was unfocused.

Roxanne shuffled through the albums until she found one marked Christmas, 1960–1970. The first picture was of Jack's mother and his father. They were standing in front of a Christmas tree in a room Roxanne recognized as the living room of this house, grinning at each other, holding hands. His dad was a slightly built man with the kindest face she'd ever seen, not much taller than Jack's mother. Obviously Jack had drawn on his forebearers' genes when it came to height. She thumbed through until she found the Christmas picture of 1963. "Jack's first Christmas," was written under the photo.

Jack's first Christmas. She knew his birthday was only

a few weeks away from now, so he was a summer baby. That made him five or six months old in this picture. Roxanne looked carefully at the old photo, taken of a family gathered around a table. She recognized Jack's aunts—so young!—and his parents, and closest to the camera, a young woman sitting with her head turned to stare back at Jack in his high chair.

There was a small dark spot visible on her neck. Roxanne felt a shiver run along her spine. The woman was the same as the one in the blurred picture taken at Easter a few years later. *Sal.*

"What's wrong?" Ginny asked, handing Roxanne a handful of purple grapes she'd systematically released from their stems.

"Nothing, sweetie," Roxanne said as she mindlessly ate the grapes.

Pansy Miller said she'd had a female boarder during December of 1963. A sickly young woman, she'd said. Someone called the blue house looking for Dolly Aames. Now there was a picture in the 1963 Wheeler photo album of a woman with a mole. True, she had dark hair in the picture instead of red, but hair color was flexible. Roxanne thumbed through the rest of the album quickly, looking for a better face shot and finally found one.

The door opened, and for a second, in the thrill of knowing Jack was home, Roxanne forgot the discovery she'd just made. She tensed her muscles to leap to her feet and throw herself into his arms.

But it wasn't Jack standing in the doorway—it was Sal.

"Ginny, Grace wants to see you," Sal began, but her voice faltered when she saw what Roxanne and Ginny were doing. Ginny put aside the Easter album and got to her feet, scattering grapes, and ran from the room. Roxanne slowly rose. She'd expected Sal to scamper away, as well, but the older woman still stood clutching the doorknob, her expression unfathomable.

Roxanne said, "We were just looking through a few picture albums."

"You were snooping."

"No. Ginny and I were just looking at old pictures of Jack. I was...interested." Her voice petered out and she felt her cheeks blaze. Did her feelings for Jack show on her reddened face? She sure felt transparent.

Sal said, "Interested in what?"

"Uh, well, Jack's family."

"Ha!"

Roxanne make a decision. She said, "You used to have a mole on the right side of your neck, didn't you?"

Sal's hand crept to her neck where she fingered what Roxanne realized was a faint white scar. She said, "Old Doc Wheeler was afraid it was dangerous so he removed it thirty some odd years ago. So what?"

"So Dolly had a mole in that exact same spot."

A tense silence filled the room.

In an intuitive leap, Roxanne added, "Did you know that in the winter of 1963, Dolly Aames's cousin called the boardinghouse in Tangent looking for her?"

Sal's eyes widened.

"Your cousin, Sal."

In a breath that was almost inaudible, Sal whispered, "Nathan? Nathan called?"

Bingo! "He called every night for a week."

"I haven't thought about him in years," Sal said softly. Then she clenched her lips tight as though willing herself to shut up.

Roxanne waited another few seconds before saying, "Why, Sal? Why did you change your name before you even hit town? Why have you been hiding all these years?"

But Sal shook her head vehemently.

"All I want to do is reassure my grandmother."

"Why does your grandmother care? It's been a long time."

"I think she feels guilty that she didn't look for you right away when a second letter didn't come. She cared for you."

"It's been a long time," Sal repeated.

Roxanne lowered her voice. "There's no way in the world I could or would even try to make you see my grandmother—that would be your decision. I just want to ease Grandma's mind. Tell me why I shouldn't tell her I found you. Tell me what I tell her when she asks how you are or wants to call you or write. Tell me how I explain the name change. If you're in trouble, if you're hiding, I don't want to cause you trouble—"

Sal interrupted. "You've done nothing but cause trouble since the moment you arrived!"

"I didn't mean to."

"Oz called early this afternoon," Sal said, her voice cold. "Your car is ready." Without another word she turned and left.

"Damn," Roxanne muttered as she sank back down to the floor. So close... However, Roxanne wasn't about to admit defeat. Eventually she turned back to the albums. Dolly Aames and Sally Collins were one and the same person. Sal had come to town in 1963, rented a room at Pansy Miller's boardinghouse, then accepted a job with the Wheeler family. She had a cousin named Nathan. Maybe his last name was the same. Nathan Collins.

The question now, of course, was why Sal had lied. She'd all but admitted she was Dolly Aames, so why not go one lousy step further and give an explanation? Why was she pretending none of it ever happened?

And most importantly, how did her lies and subterfuge, if at all, affect Jack?

An hour later, albums reshelved and assured that Ginny was napping on Grace's bed, Roxanne accepted a ride back into town from Carl. It was time to pick up her car.

Roxanne heard laughter before she even entered Oz's repair shop. Opening the door, she was struck with the sounds of a happy family. Lisa sat in a chair nursing Amy, or Sue, for that matter—the baby's toes were covered— while Oz held Sue, or Amy, over his head and lowered her to his face repeatedly to kiss her forehead.

He refused to accept any money for labor. "Heck, what with all Doc has done for me and Lisa, and most of it for free, I wouldn't feel right charging his...friend."

The pause before the word *friend* and the way Oz shuffled his feet were clear indications that the whole town was aware that she and Jack had something more than mere friendship between them. She paid the bill for the parts, then finally back in her own car, drove down Main Street.

She parked near the jewelry shop and went inside, hoping that Pansy Miller was still at the counter. She was.

"You're back!" Pansy said, looking up from a newspaper. "Is something wrong with the trophy? Say, did you bring your little girl with you?"

This time Roxanne corrected her. "Ginny isn't my little girl. I'm...well, I guess you could say I baby-sit her. And the trophy is fine. I just wanted to ask you a few questions about the woman staying at your boardinghouse when those calls for Dolly Aames came through."

"Oh, my."

"I know it's been almost forty years—"

"No, no, it's not that. I remember her clearly. Such a sad little thing."

"Sad? I thought you said she was sickly."

Pansy lowered her voice. "Sickly, sad, it's all the same, isn't it? She was depressed, I guess you'd say. She confided in me one night, swore me to confidence, and I haven't told a soul what she said, but it just about broke my heart.''

"She had a secret,'' Roxanne said, wondering how to pry it out of Pansy.

But Pansy didn't need coaxing. "It was so long ago,'' she added. "Anyway, the poor dear had had a baby out of wedlock, a big deal back then. Unfortunately the baby was born dead.''

Roxanne's breath caught. This was the tragedy in Sal's life that Jack had mentioned.

"I can't tell you how happy I was when Doc Wheeler and his wife offered her a job. They had a new baby—just what she needed, I thought. She didn't have family, you see. Both parents dead, and then the pregnancy and such a sad outcome. I have no idea if she's still around, but I bet my granddaughter could tell you.''

"That's not necessary,'' Roxanne said. She had confirmation where none was really needed, but Roxanne was trained to check and double-check her facts.

"Why do you think Doc Wheeler gave this woman a job as a housekeeper. I mean, if she was depressed and sickly—''

"You had to know Doc,'' Pansy said. "A kinder man never existed. In fact, he sent his wife, Lily, off to some distant relative's place in Northern California for most of her pregnancy. Said it was too hot down here for her. That's the kind of man he was. In fact, she had her baby up there and he joined her and brought the two of them home.''

Roxanne nodded. Jack had told her he was born in California.

"This gal I'm telling you about—Sally was her name— well, she confided in me that she'd come from up north, too.''

As Roxanne tried to assimilate all this news, she saw Jack walking toward the store.

Roxanne met Jack outside on the sidewalk. This was the first time she'd seen him since realizing the extent of her feelings for him. If only they were somewhere quiet and remote so she could touch him.

She wanted to take his hands in hers, reach up and kiss him and tell him she loved him. She wanted to feel his arms wrap around her waist as he absorbed her words. She was dying to know if it was possible he could ever return these feelings. She wanted to talk to him about their future—how they could work out the distances between them, their careers. There had to be a way.

"You're a sight for sore eyes," he told her, taking her hand and walking her to her car. "So far today, I've delivered a healthy baby boy, treated a nasty backache, diagnosed shingles, athlete's foot and a second-degree burn. Nancy Kaufman called the office—Teresa will be back day after tomorrow, so as of then, you're out of a temporary job. When I called home, I found that Grace wants out of bed right now, and Sal is in a worse mood than ever. I'm on my way home now. Sal insists she needs to talk to me. You don't know what's going on, do you?"

"Sal is upset?"

"To put it mildly." He looked down at her with his pure blue eyes, and Roxanne had an awful premonition.

She said, "Sal was angry because I was looking through your picture albums."

He shook his head. "Why would she care a hoot if you look at old pictures?"

"I'm not sure," Roxanne said. "Jack, I know about Sal's tragedy."

"She told you?"

"No, someone else did."

"I didn't know anyone else knew. Well, now you know why she won't revisit her past. Losing both a husband and a baby in a car crash really devastated her. She can't bear to think about it. I'm glad you know, I'm glad you understand.''

Roxanne kept herself from blurting out that she'd been told an entirely different story. What dead husband, what accident? What was going on?

She thought about Dolly's cousin.

Jack leaned down right then and kissed her. "Let's give the town something to talk about," he said with a grin.

"You're going to have to do better than a peck on the cheek," she whispered, still disassembling all the conflicting information.

"How about if I make love to you on that bench?"

Biting her bottom lip, she said, "Jack, you'd better go calm Sal down. I'll be home in a bit."

He leaned down close and whispered in her ear. His warm breath made her heart race—his words caused an explosion in her loins. "I finally thought of a way," he said, and the suggestive tone of his voice left no doubt about the subject matter. "Tonight we're going to take a private little drive to the art studio. If I remember correctly, all the artwork—if you could call it that—is gone, but there's a nice plush daybed. We'll be alone, Roxanne. Just you and me."

"Oh, Jack—"

"No backing out now, lover," he added.

"I have to go to the radio station and…make some calls."

"Just don't take too long," he said before kissing her on the mouth, patting her rear and walking away. At one point, he turned around and winked at her and she smiled.

How she loved him!

Now how could she protect him?

"I'm leaving," Sal said as she finished packing her suitcase. As Jack watched, she looked around her room of thirty-eight years. Apparently satisfied, she added, "I'll send for the rest of my things after I resettle."

He stood in the doorway, dazed. "You're leaving? What's going on?"

She planted her fists on her hips and replied, "I will not tolerate being spied on in what I thought was my home."

"Of course it's your home—"

"Not anymore. Not since Roxanne Salyer came snooping around."

"Sal, please, you're overreacting," Jack said, struggling to find a way to gain control over this situation. "I'll talk to Roxanne—"

"I'm sure you will. And I'm sure it will be about me. You never asked me a thing about myself until that woman showed up with all her questions."

He knew she had nowhere to go. He couldn't bear to think of her homeless, sick... He said, "I can't let you leave. Your health—"

"My health is no longer your concern."

"Tell me what you want," he said, trying hard to remain calm in the face of her ire.

"I want things the way they were before Roxanne showed up. I want you to not talk about me behind my back."

"I never do!"

She glared at him.

"Listen," he said reasonably, "I promise I won't ask you another thing about your past."

"Will Roxanne go along with that promise?"

"Roxanne doesn't have a thing to do with it. She agreed to let me talk to you—"

"She lied to you, Jack. She's been trying to corner me for days. She asked me about a mole on my neck, she was searching old albums, she's always looking at me, trying to trip me up.... She's a meddler. Okay, okay, I used to be

Dolly Aames. So what? Face it, boy, she's been using you. You do know how to pick women, don't you?''

"She wouldn't lie to me," he said. Part of his mind was spinning on one detail—Sal and Dolly were the same person?

Sal picked up her suitcase. "She's taken advantage of your kindness," she said, and stomped past him out of the room. "I won't live here and watch you make another mess of your life."

He called after her, "Sal, what about Ginny? Are you forgetting Ginny?''

The older woman turned in the hallway. "I'll never forget Ginny," she said, a sob making it into her voice. Then she turned again and hurried away. A second later, he heard the kitchen door slam, and while still stunned into inaction, the roar of Sal's car.

She was gone.

And Roxanne had caused it.

Well, what did he expect? He'd been an idiot, trusting a television producer of all people, a person driven to ferreting out every little detail no matter how many people she harmed. He'd thought she was different from Nicole—but was she? At the very least she was duplicitous and deceitful. He'd been on the brink of proposing some kind of commitment, of asking her to help him figure out a way they could continue seeing one another.

And now this.

This is what caring about a woman could do—Roxanne had single-handedly destroyed the peace in his family, a peace he'd spent the last several years securing. She'd promised to leave Sal to him, but she'd broken her word, jeopardized Sal's safety and Ginny's well-being all to satisfy her own selfish goals. Sal was Dolly? Sal had been lying? Well, so what?

All of this was his fault because none of it could have

happened if he'd kept up his guard. He'd lost control, not only of his own emotions, but of his life.

He'd trusted Roxanne....

Roxanne passed Sal's car on the drive through the desert. She waved, but Sal looked straight ahead as they slowed down to pass each other on the narrow road, and an ominous feeling started to take shape in Roxanne's gut.

By the time she reached the house, she wasn't surprised to find bedlam in the kitchen.

Jack was holding a crying Ginny. "Why didn't she say goodbye?" the child wailed, and Roxanne yearned to take her in her arms and comfort her. One look from Jack took care of that impulse. His eyes, so tender and playful just an hour or so before, were now narrowed and furious.

"Jack, what in the world—"

Grace and Carl appeared in the kitchen. "Carl told me what happened," Grace whispered. "I'm so sorry Ginny overheard us talking! Come on, Ginny. Come back to my room."

Jack nodded his thanks as Carl took Ginny from him. Grace spared Roxanne a weak smile before closing the door behind them, leaving Jack and Roxanne alone.

"Jack—"

"Sal left," he said. "You're right, she's really Dolly Aames, but you knew that already, didn't you, because you've been hounding her with questions behind my back? Go ahead, call your grandmother. I'm sure she'll be thrilled you completed your task. And that's what it was for you— a task. Destroying my family was just the by-product."

"Jack, I'm sorry. I didn't realize—"

"You didn't realize," he scoffed. "Sal is gone, Roxanne. As we both know, she's capable of disappearing from the face of the earth. She's like a grandmother to Ginny, and now, thanks to you, she's left the only home she's known in four decades. I don't think she'll ever come back.''

Roxanne swallowed the lump in her throat. She now knew the extent of Sal's secrets, but to voice them would only hurt Jack even more and she couldn't do that just to deflect his fury and pain from herself. She said, ''I didn't mean—''

''Does it matter what you meant?''

''I would hope it did,'' she said slowly.

He paused for a long moment. Roxanne could see indecision playing across his features. He finally said, ''Your boyfriend was right, Roxanne—all you care about is your own interest. *You're just like your mother.''*

His words were poison darts, his aim true. She reeled from their impact. With downcast eyes, she made her way to her room and packed her bag. When she came back to the kitchen, the room was empty. The house was silent. Roxanne let herself out the back door and looked around the now-familiar yard. Sprite and Milo stared back at her. She resisted the temptation to go over and stroke their necks, to visit the kittens and the puppies, to see Poco Oro and her mom, Goldy, just one last time.

She also fought the desire to run back inside the house to make Jack listen to her, to grab Ginny and never let go. In the end, it wasn't pride that kept her from making a scene, it was guilt.

Tears rolled down her cheeks as she drove. Jack was right—oh, not about everything, but about a lot. She'd let her ambition get in the way of her compassion. She'd allowed her fear for her grandmother to override her common sense. And worst of all, she'd managed to make everyone's life worse because she was curious.

Here she was trying to make the world a better place, applauding local heroes, and yet she'd destroyed every ounce of harmony in the home of the man she was hopelessly in love with, a man who truly did act heroic on a daily basis by taking care of the people he loved and who depended on him.

Driving back into town and checking into the motel, she decided it was time to tuck her tail between her legs. It was time to drive home as fast as she could and make someone read Gran's X rays. She had to get out of Tangent.

But not until she thought of a way to repair the damage she'd caused.

Chapter Ten

"This is the last time I'll be on the air with you," Roxanne said the next day. A plan had come to her in the wee hours of the morning. It had seemed feasible at 3:00 a.m., possible at five, but now...

The radio was the only way she had to reach out to Sal and, professional or not, she would use it.

Roxanne adjusted the volume to compensate for the fact that her voice was all but gone from crying, and added, "Teresa will be back with you tomorrow and I'll leave town and go back to Seattle where I belong. But for now, I have a special plea for a woman who means the world to a family she's just left. If she's listening, she knows who she is. I'm figuratively down on my knees. Come home. It's safe, you're loved, you're missed. The threat is over. Just come home."

Would it work? Would Sal even turn on the radio? Should she be more direct? She let it stand, adding only, "Please, for the sake of those who love you, come home."

As much as she wanted to escape as soon as her broad-

cast was finished, Roxanne had to stay at the tiny station
for another two hours, then drive to the hospital in Helpern.
It had been decided that the local hero award should be
presented by Nancy Kaufman, and since she was stuck in
a hospital bed, that's where the subdued ceremony would
take place.

Afterward, Nancy asked Roxanne to stay for a few
minutes. "I guess you must be relieved that Teresa is going
to be back tomorrow. Honestly, Roxanne, you've been ter-
rific. I wish you could stay here and be my partner forever."

Roxanne smiled, but Nancy's words were heartbreaking.
She'd loved working in the intimate atmosphere of the radio station. She'd enjoyed the one-on-one connection, the
farm reports, being part of the escalating debate over local
water rights. Even her hero contest. She'd had more op-
portunity to take risks, to grow, to affect change in these
last two weeks than in the last two years in Seattle.

She said, "You have a great little station. I enjoyed every
moment. Thank you."

Nancy caught her hand. "I heard you this morning."

Roxanne immediately felt contrite. "Nancy, I'm sorry. I
wouldn't have used the airwaves for my personal problems
except that I didn't know what else to do."

"I wondered if you and Jack...well, if Jack and you..."

"No," Roxanne said.

Nancy smiled. "I just hoped."

As Roxanne drove back to Tangent and past the radio
station, she wondered how she'd allowed herself to become
so involved in this town. She'd spent so little time in Tangent, and yet it felt like home, the people here felt like
family. Would she ever recapture this feeling somewhere
else? How could she? There might be other towns, but there
was only one Jack and one Ginny, and not only was she
leaving them, but they hated her.

Her heart felt like the expanse of desert outside her car windows: dry, lonely, desolate. Once back at the motel and inside her room, she collapsed on the sagging bed. Grief stricken the night before, she hadn't slept. Fatigue caught up with her. One moment, she was staring at the ceiling, planning on taking off in the cool of the evening, and the next she was waking up in a darkened room. Someone was knocking at the door.

Jack!

It had to be him. Who else? He'd thought about what he'd said. He'd decided she wasn't awful after all. He'd come to apologize, or at least to listen to her apology. He'd realized he needed her, that he loved her.

All this ran through her mind as she rushed to open the door.

Sal stood on the threshold.

Roxanne couldn't help but look behind the diminutive woman who seemed to have shrunk even more in the hours since Roxanne had last seen her.

"I saw your car out front," Sal said.

Roxanne turned away from the door.

Sal stood just inside with the door still open. "I heard you on the air," she added.

"Then you know I'm leaving Tangent. It's safe for you to go home. Jack and Ginny need you."

"I can't go back," Sal said as tears began rolling down her cheeks. "There's too much at stake."

"Like your pride?"

"No, more than that. Roxanne, I have to know. How much did you tell Jack?"

Roxanne sank down on the edge of the motel bed. "I didn't tell Jack anything."

"But *you* know," Sal said, and she seemed relieved somehow.

"I know you're Dolly Aames. I know you came here

under an assumed name in 1963, wrote a brief note to my grandmother with plans to write again, then decided to disappear. I know you told conflicting stories about your past. I had to ask myself why. So I used the computer at the radio station and typed in the name Nathan Collins, a possibility for your cousin's name. I tried Washington and Oregon. I found him in California. In Arcata, California.''

"I didn't know he was still alive," Sal whispered, tears running down her cheeks.

"Alive and still practicing law. I called him. He was so relieved to hear you were okay that he divulged a lot of information he probably shouldn't have. Sal, I know you gave birth in July of 1963 in Arcata. That's the same place Jack's mother went to have her baby.''

Sal flinched.

"I know your son was born alive and that your cousin had a hand in placing him. I can't find one picture of Jack's mother pregnant. So I visited Sadie and Veronica. The two of them fell all over themselves contradicting each other about her due date, about which relative she stayed with. It's impossible not to reach certain conclusions, but I think you are the only one around here who knows who Jack's birth mother really is.''

Sal covered her mouth with trembling fingers.

"But none of this matters," Roxanne said. "Your secrets are safe, I promise. I will never say a word about any of it to Jack.''

Silent sobs shook the older woman's body, then erupted into a moan of despair that made Roxanne shudder. Roxanne's heart went out to her.

Eventually Sal wiped at her eyes and cleared her throat. Though tears still rolled down her cheeks, she started talking. "There was a man," she said softly. "He was the husband of one of the other singers. His name was Ken Bender. He was older and worldly and he said his marriage was finished. I was nineteen at the time and stupid as a rock. When I got pregnant, he gave me money. I thought he wanted to marry me—he promised—but he didn't. He said he still loved his wife and he wanted me to disappear.''

"But you had friends. Grandma, for instance—"

"She would have been disgusted with me, Roxanne. I'd been having an affair with a married man—the husband of one of my friends, one of Nell's friends. I couldn't tell her or anyone else. My parents were gone—there just wasn't anyone but my cousin in Arcata.''

Roxanne wanted to tell Sal she didn't have to say another word, but Sal appeared to need to get her story out in the open. Perhaps this was a catharsis. If so, it had been a long time coming.

Sal continued, her voice subdued but determined. "I went to my cousin's place. As you know, he is a lawyer. He knew of a couple who desperately wanted a baby but couldn't conceive one of their own. The woman had contacted everyone in the state for a private adoption, so my cousin said it was like fate. When the baby was born, he handled the adoption, but I hounded him until he told me the man's profession and the town they came from. I had to know who had my baby. For a while, I thought I could live with it, but then I found I couldn't. I moved here using an assumed name. There was only one doctor in town, so finding my baby was easy. At first, I just wanted to assure myself that they were decent people. Then Doc Wheeler offered me a job. When Jack's adoptive mother died, I stayed on and mothered him.''

"And the family never told Jack he was adopted and that you were his mother?"

"They didn't know I was his mother. No one knew that but my cousin. And no one in Tangent but Sadie and Veronica even knew Jack was adopted. I think they kind of suspected that Jack was more to me that just another child,

but they never asked and I never told a soul—until now.''
Sal took a step forward, her face crumbling in slow motion.
''And now because of you and your prying, I've lost Jack,''
she cried, tumbling into Roxanne's arms. ''I've lost my
son.''

Roxanne looked over the white head of the woman
weeping in her arms and met Jack's piercing gaze. The look
in his eyes made it clear he'd heard every single word.

''Your son?'' he whispered.

Sal jerked upright in a flash. Turning to face Jack, she
swallowed her own tears and reached out a hand.

''You're my mother?''

''Jack—''

''No!'' he said. ''My mother is dead. This is all some
crazy fabrication.''

Roxanne thought that a weaker man, a lesser man, would
have stumbled away, would have fled the truth that shook
everything he'd always believed about himself. But Jack
stood there, staring at Sal. She could see his emotions racing across his face.

''I never wanted to hurt you,'' Sal cried.

''Then this is true?''

Sal nodded.

''My aunts knew? My dad and mom? And no one told
me that I was adopted? Everything I thought I am is a lie,
a fabrication? You're my mother, Sal?''

She nodded. Neither Jack nor Sal made a move. Roxanne
extricated herself from under Sal and went to Jack. She
took both of his hands, rubbing them with hers, trying to
put some life back into him. Her heart was bursting with
love, her head throbbing with the need to offer him help.
If he would take it from her.

''It really doesn't change who you are,'' Roxanne murmured. ''Jack, you had two mothers who loved you. You
had two aunts who wanted to shield you. You had a father

who adored you and wanted you to follow in his footsteps. And you have Sal, a woman who cared enough about you to try to protect you from discovering something that would have made her life easier and your life more difficult. You were raised in a home full of love. You turned out strong and kind and wonderful.''

"But—"

"Yes, *but*. All right, *but*. You have reason to feel disgruntled, you have cause to be upset. No one likes to have the wool pulled over their eyes, and that's how you're feeling right now. But that wasn't the intention. Those weren't even the facts. You were offered unconditional love and security. You were a part of a real family.''

He stared at Roxanne for a second, his eyes still bewildered, his mouth still stern, then he dropped her hands. She felt like collapsing once the connection was severed. She had a feeling it was the last time she would ever touch him.

He went to Sal. She had buried her face in her hands and was still crying. Gently he helped her to stand, then with one last unfathomable look at Roxanne, he ushered his mother out of the room.

Roxanne closed the door behind them and wanted to die.

"I'm on my way back to Seattle," she told her grandmother the next morning.

"Your voice sounds funny. Have you caught a cold?''

"No. I'll be home in two days and I'll storm that hospital and get your X rays released to another doctor. This is ridiculous. I won't stand for it!''

Grandma Nell coughed. "Too late," she said. "The doctor came back yesterday and read the X rays. He thinks I may be allergic to Linda's parrot.''

Roxanne began crying.

"Honey, didn't you hear me? I'm okay!''

The tears kept rolling. Tears of relief for Gran, of loss for herself. "I'm just so happy."

"Now listen, did you ever find Dolly?"

Roxanne had agonized about how to answer this question. She said, "Yes and no. I'll tell you about it in a couple of days."

"Well, I hope you got a nice vacation out of it anyway."

Roxanne couldn't bring herself to respond. What could she say? *I'm coming home with half my heart? I'm never going to be truly happy again?* She said, "I'll see you very soon."

While filling her car with gas at the station next to Oz's garage the next morning, she heard that Sal had returned home. "Carl and one of the hands came in to get her car down at the motel where she left it," Oz told her. He'd wandered over to see how the car was running. "Wonder what the old gal was doing at the motel?" This last question was accompanied by a pair of raised eyebrows.

Roxanne shrugged.

Sal was home. "Mission accomplished," Roxanne whispered to herself as she drove out of town. It wasn't her original mission, she didn't even know if she'd made things better or worse. All she knew was that she missed the animals, the ranch, Ginny.

And that she would miss Jack for the rest of her life.

Jack, dressed in his jeans, old shirt and favorite Stetson, rode Milo across the desert. The horse was a pro at finding footing in the sand, skirting gullies and dodging tumbleweed. Jack could see the dark ribbon of highway up ahead, and for one gut-wrenching moment, he thought he might be too late. There was a white car speeding away from town.

No, it was too big a car to be hers. Or at least he hoped it was.

He kept going. After Oz called, he knew he could never catch her by driving into town—his only hope lay over the rough terrain. Within minutes, he was beside the road. Milo shook his head and whinnied and sure enough, another white dot appeared on the horizon in the direction of Tangent.

He waited.

Roxanne slowed down as she recognized the man astride the brown horse. Hope leapt in her chest, but she fought it back with determination. Just because he was here didn't mean anything more than his wanting to settle things between them. Still, as she pulled the car far off the road and opened the door, her heart danced through her innards.

He got off the horse and looped the reins around an old section of broken fence.

They stared at one another. Roxanne could hardly breathe. The air seemed heavy and hot and she was reminded of the day he'd found her out in the desert, lost and scared.

"I had to thank you," he said at last.

This wasn't what she expected. She said, "Thank me? For what? Ruining your life?"

He smiled at her and moved closer. She steeled herself against the involuntary reaction her body had to his.

"You didn't ruin my life," he said, stopping a couple of feet away from her. "You helped me in kind of a hard moment back there at the motel. I've given a lot of thought to what you had to say. Besides, thanks to you and your meddling, Sal has come out of the closet, so to speak. She seems happier than I've ever seen her. It's good."

Roxanne shook her head. "This is rich, you thanking me after all I've done."

"You are a scared little thing," he said suddenly, touching her cheek with one finger.

"I'm not scared. I'm...well, a busybody, I guess. You were right—"

"Hogwash. Let me tell you something about yourself, Roxanne."

"Oh, please, do."

He grinned. "Ever since the day you got to town, you've been looking out for other people. First there was Ginny and then Grace and Lisa and Oz and the twins and Nancy Kaufman and Tony—I can't keep them all straight. But you've stood up and been counted while you were here, and I admire that. I have to ask myself why you acted so selflessly."

"I didn't," she snapped. "You pointed out my self-serving reasons. I was manipulating you and your family. I was using the town and my feminine wiles to get you to relax so I could ravage your life."

"Ouch," he said, wincing.

She laughed. What she wanted to do was cry. She said, "You were right about me, Jack."

"No, honey," he said, stepping closer still, "I was all wrong about you. I mean, I was right at the beginning, but I let my own fears and weaknesses get in the way. I mistrusted you for all the wrong reasons. I hope you can forgive me."

Tears were building behind her nose. How could he be so oblivious to the way she felt about him? She said, "Well, it all turned out okay. How is Ginny?"

"Funniest thing. She's been carrying around her little ballerina box and making wishes that you would come back. Then she gave me a penny." He dug in his pocket and came up with a spot of copper. "What's this all about?"

Roxanne stared at the penny. "It's a secret," she said at last.

He shook his head, took off his hat and tugged it on

again. "Roxanne, I can't begin to tell you what it meant to me to see your car parked out in front of the motel last night. Haven't you wondered why I came to your room?"

"I assumed you heard me on the radio."

"That's right. When I heard your voice, I realized I'd acted like a jerk. I couldn't let you leave like that."

"Well, I appreciate your coming out here to tell me."

"I can't imagine why a woman like you would want to spend the rest of her life in a place like this," he said, the suggestion of blue flashing from under the brim of his hat.

She shrugged. "This town isn't so bad. There's hardly ever a parking problem."

"That's true. And traffic isn't too bad."

"Unless you hit rush hour."

"Then there's our fried chicken at the Handy-Mart. It hasn't actually killed anyone—well, not that I know of."

She just stared at him. She wasn't sure what he was trying to say.

"You see," he said, looking to his right as a truck rumbled past, waving a hand when the truck honked a greeting. "You see, I was just wondering if you've ever given any thought to where you'd like to go on a honeymoon."

Roxanne was sure the noise of the truck had distorted his words. She said, "What?"

"You know, a honeymoon. I was thinking of a place like Niagara Falls. I hear there's a state park on the United States side that's really something. I was wondering if there's a woman alive who would actually like to go camping for her honeymoon."

She hadn't misheard all of that! Was he asking her—she couldn't bear to think it in case she was wrong.

Cupping her face in his hands, he added, "I told you once that I had everything a man could want, but I was wrong. Last night I realized that for the first time in my life, I am hopelessly, head over heels in love. I'm not going to walk away from this chance, Roxanne, unless you don't love me in return.''

Putting her hands over his, she kissed his fingers. "Oh, Jack—"

"I'll be honest. I can't move to Seattle. This place is a part of me. The people here need a doctor and I can't think of anyone else crazy enough to stay around for them. I don't want to date for weeks and months and years with you flying down here sometimes and me flying up there. I need you now. I want you here, in my house, in my bed. I think you are my last great chance for happiness, Ginny's too. I think I can make you happy. Hell, Roxanne, I love you.''

"I must be dreaming," Roxanne said as tears flooded her eyes.

"Oh, now, don't cry," he said wiping them away with his fingers. "I hate it when people cry." He leaned down and stopped her tears by kissing her tenderly, profoundly, with a promise in every caress of his hands, in every warm breath against her skin.

"But Sal—"

"What about Sal?"

"She hates me. She won't want me living in her home—"

"Shh," he said, kissing her again. "Sal doesn't hate you. You've freed her from four decades of lies. She's Ginny's grandmother, and though she may never want to tell her that, I know it means something to her to know that I know.''

"And she's your mother."

"That takes some getting used to. I may need help adjusting to that. But, Roxanne, this isn't about Sal. This is about you and me and Ginny. The real question is this. Can you be happy here with just a little radio station to fill your professional ambitions?''

"Jack, that isn't a consideration. I love that radio station and Nancy needs me."

He nodded. "Then answer me this. Do you want to take on the ranch, the people, the animals and most importantly, me and Ginny? Will you stay here forever? Because that's what I'm talking about, Roxanne—forever."

"I want a baby," Roxanne whispered.

"As many as you want," he whispered back. "Just don't ask me to have your portrait painted."

"I love you," she added. "I can't believe this is happening. I realized a couple of days ago that everything I wanted in life was embodied in one person—you."

He kissed her yet again, and Roxanne felt the pieces of her life slipping into place.

Jack swept her up into his arms, took a few bold steps, then stopped. They smiled at each other. There was really nowhere for them to go, no way to stay together at that moment. Roxanne had a car and he had a horse and they were miles from anywhere.

"Look," she said, pointing out into the desert as a mother quail and her babies scurried across the sand. "How perfect is that?" she said, meeting his gaze. Then slowly she raised her face to his and touched his lips. This time the heat they generated together made the desert seem like an oasis in comparison.

"Lock your car. I'll send someone to get it later," he said at last. "You're coming with me."

Roxanne did as directed. He mounted his horse, then freeing the left stirrup so she could find a foothold, reached down and pulled her up behind him. As he nudged the horse forward, Roxanne wrapped her arms around his firm torso and rested her cheek against his sunbathed back.

They rode in the direction of the ranch.

They rode home.

Epilogue

Grandma Nell had a new yellow hat to match her new yellow dress. The other Sunflowers were also wearing yellow though it was radio and there was only a small audience waiting to toast their performance with cake and punch.

Ginny had pulled a chair up close to the glass so she could peer in at the four elderly women getting ready to sing. Nancy Kaufman, baby boy on her lap, announced them, using the script Roxanne had written. Nothing in the introduction hinted at the tumultuous and fateful trip this group had taken to reunite for this one last song.

"They all look so cute, don't they?" Grace said. Her baby, a little girl she'd named Samantha, was asleep in Carl's arms.

"They look happy," Roxanne said. *And healthy...*

Sal waved at Ginny. Then her gaze found Roxanne's and she smiled.

Tears filled Roxanne's eyes.

Jack said, "Don't start crying, honey."

"I'm pregnant," Roxanne said. "All I do anymore is eat and cry."

He laughed. Suddenly the introduction was over and Nancy hit the button that started the prerecorded music playing. The Sunflowers, in perfect harmony, sang.

At that moment Roxanne felt a fluttering deep inside her body and knew that she'd just felt the first movements of her child. Reaching behind her, she wrapped Jack's arms around her stomach so that his hands rested on her abdomen.

"What's wrong?" Jack whispered in her ear.

"The baby just moved. Maybe he'll be a singer like his great-grandmother."

"And his grandmother," Jack added, kissing the top of her head.

Closing her eyes, Roxanne leaned back against her husband and let the music wash through her soul.

* * * * *

Feel like a star with Silhouette.

We will fly you and a guest to New York City for an exciting weekend stay at a glamorous 5-star hotel. Experience a refreshing day at one of New York's trendiest spas and have your photo taken by a professional. Plus, receive $1,000 U.S. spending money!

**Flowers...long walks...dinner for two...
how does Silhouette Books
make romance come alive for you?**

Send us a script, with 500 words or less, along with visuals (only drawings, magazine cutouts or photographs or combination thereof). Show us how Silhouette Makes Your Love Come Alive. Be creative and have fun. No purchase necessary. All entries must be clearly marked with your name, address and telephone number. All entries will become property of Silhouette and are not returnable. **Contest closes September 28, 2001.**

Please send your entry to: **Silhouette Makes You a Star!**

In U.S.A.	In Canada
P.O. Box 9069	P.O. Box 637
Buffalo, NY, 14269-9069	Fort Erie, ON, L2A 5X3

Look for contest details on the next page, by visiting www.eHarlequin.com or request a copy by sending a self-addressed envelope to the applicable address above. Contest open to Canadian and U.S. residents who are 18 or over. Void where prohibited.

Silhouette®
Where love comes alive™

Our lucky winner's photo will appear in a Silhouette ad. Join the fun!

SRMYAS1

HARLEQUIN "SILHOUETTE MAKES YOU A STAR!" CONTEST 1308
OFFICIAL RULES
NO PURCHASE NECESSARY TO ENTER

1. To enter, follow directions published in the offer to which you are responding. Contest begins June 1, 2001, and ends on September 28, 2001. Entries must be postmarked by September 28, 2001, and received by October 5, 2001. Enter by hand-printing (or typing) on an 8 ½" x 11" piece of paper your name, address (including zip code), contest number/name and attaching a script containing 500 words or less, along with drawings, photographs or magazine cutouts, or combinations thereof (i.e., collage) on no larger than 9" x 12" piece of paper, describing how the Silhouette books make romance come alive for you. Mail via first-class mail to: Harlequin "Silhouette Makes You a Star!" Contest 1308, (in the U.S.) P.O. Box 9069, Buffalo, NY 14269-9069, (in Canada) P.O. Box 637, Fort Erie, Ontario, Canada L2A 5X3. Limit one entry per person, household or organization.

2. Contests will be judged by a panel of members of the Harlequin editorial, marketing and public relations staff. Fifty percent of criteria will be judged against script and fifty percent will be judged against drawing, photographs and/or magazine cutouts. Judging criteria will be based on the following:

   - Sincerity—25%
   - Originality and Creativity—50%
   - Emotionally Compelling—25%

   In the event of a tie, duplicate prizes will be awarded. Decisions of the judges are final.

3. All entries become the property of Torstar Corp. and may be used for future promotional purposes. Entries will not be returned. No responsibility is assumed for lost, late, illegible, incomplete, inaccurate, nondelivered or misdirected mail.

4. Contest open only to residents of the U.S. (except Puerto Rico) and Canada who are 18 years of age or older, and is void wherever prohibited by law; all applicable laws and regulations apply. Any litigation within the Province of Quebec respecting the conduct or organization of a publicity contest may be submitted to the Régie des alcools, des courses et des jeux for a ruling. Any litigation respecting the awarding of a prize may be submitted to the Régie des alcools, des courses et des jeux only for the purpose of helping the parties reach a settlement. Employees and immediate family members of Torstar Corp. and D. L. Blair, Inc., their affiliates, subsidiaries and all other agencies, entities and persons connected with the use, marketing or conduct of this contest are not eligible to enter. Taxes on prizes are the sole responsibility of the winner. Acceptance of any prize offered constitutes permission to use winner's name, photograph or other likeness for the purposes of advertising, trade and promotion on behalf of Torstar Corp., its affiliates and subsidiaries without further compensation to the winner, unless prohibited by law.

5. Winner will be determined no later than November 30, 2001, and will be notified by mail. Winner will be required to sign and return an Affidavit of Eligibility/Release of Liability/Publicity Release form within 15 days after winner notification. Noncompliance within that time period may result in disqualification and an alternative winner may be selected. All travelers must execute a Release of Liability prior to ticketing and must possess required travel documents (e.g., passport, photo ID) where applicable. Trip must be booked by December 31, 2001, and completed within one year of notification. No substitution of prize permitted by winner. Torstar Corp. and D. L. Blair, Inc., their parents, affiliates and subsidiaries are not responsible for errors in printing of contest, entries and/or game pieces. In the event of printing or other errors that may result in unintended prize values or duplication of prizes, all affected game pieces or entries shall be null and void. **Purchase or acceptance of a product offer does not improve your chances of winning.**

6. Prizes: (1) Grand Prize—A 2-night/3-day trip for two (2) to New York City, including round-trip coach air transportation nearest winner's home and hotel accommodations (double occupancy) at The Plaza Hotel, a glamorous afternoon makeover at a trendy New York spa, $1,000 in U.S. spending money and an opportunity to have a professional photo taken and appear in a Silhouette advertisement (approximate retail value: $7,000). (10) Ten Runner-Up Prizes of gift packages (retail value $50 ea.). Prizes consist of only those items listed as part of the prize. Limit one prize per person. Prize is valued in U.S. currency.

7. For the name of the winner (available after December 31, 2001) send a self-addressed, stamped envelope to: Harlequin "Silhouette Makes You a Star!" Contest 1197 Winners, P.O. Box 4200 Blair, NE 68009-4200 or you may access the www.eHarlequin.com Web site through February 28, 2002.

Contest sponsored by Torstar Corp., P.O Box 9042, Buffalo, NY 14269-9042.

SRMYAS2

If you enjoyed what you just read,
then we've got an offer you can't resist!

Take 2 bestselling
love stories FREE!
Plus get a FREE surprise gift!

Clip this page and mail it to Silhouette Reader Service™

IN U.S.A.
3010 Walden Ave.
P.O. Box 1867
Buffalo, N.Y. 14240-1867

IN CANADA
P.O. Box 609
Fort Erie, Ontario
L2A 5X3

YES! Please send me 2 free Silhouette Romance® novels and my free surprise gift. Then send me 6 brand-new novels every month, which I will receive months before they're available in stores. In the U.S.A., bill me at the bargain price of $2.90 plus 25¢ delivery per book and applicable sales tax, if any*. In Canada, bill me at the bargain price of $3.25 plus 25¢ delivery per book and applicable taxes**. That's the complete price and a savings of at least 10% off the cover prices—what a great deal! I understand that accepting the 2 free books and gift places me under no obligation ever to buy any books. I can always return a shipment and cancel at any time. Even if I never buy another book from Silhouette, the 2 free books and gift are mine to keep forever. So why not take us up on our invitation. You'll be glad you did!

215 SEN C24Q
315 SEN C24R

Name	(PLEASE PRINT)	
Address	Apt.#	
City	State/Prov.	Zip/Postal Code

* Terms and prices subject to change without notice. Sales tax applicable in N.Y.
** Canadian residents will be charged applicable provincial taxes and GST.
All orders subject to approval. Offer limited to one per household.
® are registered trademarks of Harlequin Enterprises Limited.

SROM00_R   ©1998 Harlequin Enterprises Limited